Powerful Teacher Learning

What the Theatre Arts Teach about Collaboration

DAVID ALLEN

ROWMAN & LITTLEFIELD EDUCATION
A Division of
ROWMAN & LITTLEFIELD PUBLISHERS, INC.
Lanham • New York • Toronto • Plymouth, UK

Published by Rowman & Littlefield Education
A division of Rowman & Littlefield Publishers, Inc.
A wholly owned subsidiary of The Rowman & Littlefield Publishing Group, Inc.
4501 Forbes Boulevard, Suite 200, Lanham, Maryland 20706
www.rowman.com

10 Thornbury Road, Plymouth PL6 7PP, United Kingdom

British Library Cataloguing in Publication Information Available

Library of Congress Cataloging-in-Publication Data

Allen, David, 1961-
Powerful teacher learning : what the theatre arts teach about collaboration / David Allen.
pages cm
Includes bibliographical references.
ISBN 978-1-61048-681-1 (cloth : alk. paper) — ISBN 978-1-61048-682-8 (pbk. : alk. paper) — ISBN 978-1-61048-683-5 (electronic) 1. Teachers—In-service training—United States. 2. Teachers—Professional relationships—United States. 3. Professional learning communities—United States. 4. Theater—Study and teaching—United States. 5. Drama in education—United States. I. Title.
LB1731.A448 2013
370.71'1—dc23

2013012115

∞™ The paper used in this publication meets the minimum requirements of American National Standard for Information Sciences—Permanence of Paper for Printed Library Materials, ANSI/NISO Z39.48-1992.

Printed in the United States of America

Contents

Foreword

Four Moves toward an Artistry of Teaching

STEVE SEIDEL
Patricia Bauman and John Landrum Bryant Lecturer on Arts in Education, Harvard Graduate School of Eduction

1. FROM IMAGES TO REALITIES

Over fifteen years ago, Amelia Gambetti, the first educator I met from the remarkable preschools in Reggio Emilia, Italy, introduced me to three questions that the teachers in those schools often asked themselves:

- What is your image of the child?
- What is your image of the teacher?
- What is your image of the school?

For Amelia and her colleagues, these questions—and how we answer them—are a powerful starting point for any consideration of what does, what can, and what should happen in classrooms and schools. My own thinking about schools and schooling has been profoundly changed by my encounters with the Reggio schools, and these questions have been especially provocative. Of course, we all have our own answers to these questions, and nobody else can answer them for us.

In each case, these questions ask us to consider and articulate how we really see each of these critical elements of the educational enterprise. Do we see children, for example, as cute? Vulnerable? As empty vessels waiting to be filled? Or, perhaps, as curious and capable? Do we see them as researchers? As citizens? And so on. Whatever our answers, our images of children (and teachers and schools), all of which surely have multiple dimensions, have a powerful influence on how we understand and approach our work as teachers and how we design schools for us all to work, play, and learn in.

In a sense, these are the questions that David Allen has posed in this radical book. As he notes early in the book, educators—as well as non-educators who are concerned about the state of our schools—look for images, models, and practices from other fields to inspire and guide educational practice. They draw analogies and create metaphors to clarify and enrich their thinking. If these are taken seriously, the implications of those images, analogies, and metaphors can be quite deep and powerful.

Going back at least two decades, many educators had a fascination with the use of "total quality management" (TQM), a practice developed by Toyota in the manufacture of automobiles, for the improvement of public schools (Lunenburg, 2010). In the third edition of his influential book, *Total Quality Management in Education*, Sallis (2002) argues, "It is instructive to look to the business world for an insight into quality. IBM's definition puts it simply: 'quality equals customer satisfaction'" (p. 2). This suggests another question to add to Reggio's three: What is your image of quality in education? In that context, it could be informative to examine the implications of this particular business model in relation to educational settings, goals, and relationships.

Allen notes the practice of examining other professional domains, such as clinical psychology, ministry, and medicine, for both comparative purposes (how we do in education compared to these other fields) and for borrowing best practices. This can be productive and has spawned all sorts of initiatives in teacher professional development, such as the use of the various models of medical "rounds" as inspiration for comparable practices with public school teachers. In each of these cases, it is important to consider the appropriateness of the analogy. Just how is medicine or ministry or clinical psychology actually like teaching—and how might they be significantly different?

The human imagination is a very powerful force. Analogies and metaphors are expressions of our imaginative capacity to link two otherwise disconnected elements. They help us to see one element in relation to our image of the other. This can be benign, but it can also be extremely generative or destructive. I believe this is why Amelia Gambetti's colleagues keep returning to their three "images questions" for reexamination and reconsideration. Anyone using an analogy about teachers, students, and schools should do so only after reading the warning on the label: USE WITH EXTREME CAUTION. YOU WILL LIKELY CREATE JUST WHAT YOU IMAGINE.

2. FROM ANALOGIES TO PRACTICES

An analogy announces a connection to explore for deeper resonances and the possibility that each element may illuminate and inform our understanding of the other. To make an analogy requires both a strong feeling for the deep structure and nature of the two things being linked and a leap of imagination.

Early in this book, Allen acknowledges that other educators and scholars have explored analogous dimensions of theatre and teaching. As he notes in chapter 3, "While some of these are constrained by either a tight focus on the individual teacher or a limited appreciation of theatre arts practices, others demonstrate the potential for a broader and deeper dialogue across the domains of theatre and teacher learning in groups—a potential this book seeks to exploit." Indeed, an analogy deeply analyzed may well suggest ways in which we might quite radically reconceive the way we work in either realm. In other words, analogies, when taken seriously, have the potential to change practice.

Sometimes we live so close to two analogous realms that, although we might live in their connections, we somehow can't get a clear view of the relationship, which is why, in personal terms, I'm so glad David Allen wrote this book. The worlds of theatre and teaching that he explores are worlds with which I have long professional associations and for which I have great affection and respect. I'm not speaking only of theatre and education broadly, but of the quite specific sub-worlds of avant-garde theatre companies that engage in creating original works or highly interpretive takes on classic texts and the still relatively small, though growing, movement to create teacher collectives, most often within schools, though sometimes across schools, for the examination and improvement of teaching practice—teacher learning groups, or TLGs, as they are called here.

In the spirit of full disclosure, David Allen and I worked together at Project Zero, a research group at the Harvard Graduate School of Education, from 1998 to 2002, on several projects dedicated to creating TLGs, or "teacher inquiry groups," as we called them then. I was aware in those years that Allen was fascinated by theatre and especially the practices of such avant-garde artists as Jerzy Grotowski, Peter Brook, Anne Bogart, and others.

Starting in my teens, I had worked as an actor and then became a high school theatre teacher and also a stage director. Inspired by productions directed by Peter Brook and especially by his creation of the International Centre of Theatre Research in Paris in 1970, I moved, over the years, further and further in my own work from traditional productions of plays to much more developmental rehearsal processes ("collective creation," as it is referred to here) and experimental performances. I followed the work of avant-garde theatre artists, such as Richard Foreman, The Wooster Group, and the San Francisco Mime Troupe, and I was blessed to study for several years with Lee Breuer and Ruth Malaczech, two of the founding members of Mabou Mines.

I was always fascinated by the ways in which theatre artists like Grotowski and Brook, back in the 1960s and 1970s, were appropriating the language of research and science to signal their embrace of qualities in their work that were not so often associated with the theatre. Yes, I thought, theatre can—and should—be a process of rigorous examination of human nature, language, emotional truths, the body, and even the processes through which art, particularly theatre, accrues its power. The relationship to an established script as the foundation for making theatre was also being challenged in this kind of theatre work. The script was no longer sacred; the actors no longer limited to faithful, classical representations of the text. Either the text was being fully invented by the theatre company or in collaboration with a contemporary playwright or a classic text was being entirely reinterpreted.

In the same years that I was enamored of this kind of theatre work, I began teaching. Though influenced by the work of other educators, my colleagues and I created our own lessons and units of study in our alternative high school. We also often taught in teams, usually in pairs, but sometimes in groups of three or four, and we thought of the staff as a collective. It was a brand-new school and we were creators of the school, just as we were creators of its curriculum and instructional approaches.

In retrospect, since I certainly didn't have this language at that time, I can see that we were engaged in collective creation, constantly analyzing what was and wasn't working in our classrooms and making adjustments and changes. Dialogue and debate about teaching was constant—both within formal meetings and then spilling into every corner of the school day and our lives outside the building.

All of this was scrappy. We didn't have the perspective, vision, or analytic perseverance that Allen brings to this book. Few teachers ever do. Teachers, like those in any complex professional world, are often dependent on their dialogue with researchers and scholars working in other settings and with different influences for the insights that their thinking—and, to be sure, their analogic leaps of imagination—provides. Just as researchers and scholars are so deeply dependent on teachers—and, in this case, artists—for their insights and understandings.

In this case, the analogies and metaphors are only Allen's starting point. He has gone much further in his analysis of Bogart, Anna Halprin, Liz Lerman, and other theatre artists to create and offer a set of frameworks and practices to guide the work of TLGs. He has extracted the concepts of "means," "materials," and "modes" from the work of the theatre companies he has studied to provide provocations for reconceiving the practices of TLGs.

"Means" captures the various "structures groups employ to initiate and guide their processes of collective creation." "Materials" include the diverse resources teachers and their colleagues bring to the work of the TLG, including curricula, student work, assessment practices, and so on, including, I would add, their extensive and deep knowledge of their individual students and their "pedagogical content knowledge" (Shulman, 1987).

Finally and critically, he offers the idea of "modes of engagement"—a way of discussing the orientation and cultures of "collective creators," whether in theatre companies or TLGs. He suggests a profound shift for many TLGs as he draws from the "modes" of the theatre artists he studied—a shift in which the "modes of *exploration* and *composition* replace more familiar modes of problem-solving or evaluation" (my italics).

3. FROM PRACTICES TO "PRODUCTS-AS-PERFORMANCES"

As the move from images to practices is envisioned in this book, teachers become explorers and composers and this leads to a third move toward a conception of teaching that sees artistry as an essential element of the work. In chapter 1, Allen explains, "While recognizing the 'generative power evident in metaphor [of theatrical performance]' (Egan, 1997, p. 55), in this book, I focus on the specific *practices* of theatre artists. I try to understand how these practices generate the *performances* that are the company's products and relate this understanding to the practices and products of TLGs." Allen sees the work of teachers—and TLGs—in very unusual terms.

First, he sees their work as collective. Anyone who has spent time in public schools knows that, overwhelmingly, teaching is an individual and often extremely isolating enterprise. Do we retreat to our classrooms or are we confined there with schedules that provide precious few moments during the day, week, or, for many, the month to truly engage in any collaboration with our colleagues down the hall or even next door to us?

There is no need to argue the debilitating effects of this isolation. It is one of the preeminent and most destructive ways in which teaching is not treated as a real profession. This book starts from the premise that teaching, like theatre, is a collective activity, whether the teacher is alone with her students in the classroom or the actress is performing a monologue. There are always others who inform and influence the "performance."

Second, Allen's analogy to theatre suggests that the work of TLGs is a creative activity that yields two kinds of products-as-performances—"instructional and conceptual resources"—that are explained and explored throughout the book. This, too, is a radical concept in a field where so many who don't teach, but do have power—our so-called educational leaders, from school administrators to school boards, philanthropists to publishers, and politicians to the media—call and argue for "teacher-proof" curriculum and instructional materials. (The "education-industrial complex"—the publishers and testing and professional development industries—always stands ready to protect children and taxpayers from the incompetence of teachers with their "foolproof" products and services.)

In the discourse around contemporary public education, teachers are rarely seen as creative or innovative. In Allen's view, though, a radical restructuring and reconceptualization of schools and teaching, informed by the image of teachers as collective creators, is a step toward restoring both significant responsibilities and some dignity to the work of teaching.

4. FROM CRAFT TO ARTISTRY

No less than Bill Gates, founder and director of the largest foundation in the world, offered his conclusion, in 2009, about what's wrong and what must be done to improve educational outcomes. "We need to identify effective behaviors [of great teachers] so we can transfer those skills to other teachers. It is amazing how little [a] data-driven approach to teacher effectiveness has been taken" (Barret, 2009).

And there to answer his call was Doug Lemov, a popular education writer and school administrator, who, with the identification of forty-nine "techniques," has distilled what it takes to "teach like a champion."

> Imagine a classroom where the same students who, moments before, were unruly and undisciplined suddenly take their seats, pull out their notebooks and as if by magic, think and work like scholars. In a time of massive education budget cuts and layoffs, this scenario seems unlikely. Yet in classrooms around the U.S. there stands one teacher—an artisan whose techniques and execution differentiates her from her peers. What is this teacher's secret? Does she possess an innate talent for the trade, or can her craft be learned? (Lemov, 2010)

To be sure, Lemov answers his own question over and over: the craft can be learned. This is heartening in two ways. First, that he sees teaching as a craft and, second, that essentially anyone can learn it with, Lemov adds, practice and critique.

It is interesting to return to the idea of images and ask the Reggio "image question" of Lemov and so many others who have embraced his work: "What is your image of the teacher?" (Indeed, it seems similarly important to ask about his image of a scholar.) Just drawing from this short quote, it seems Lemov sees the teacher as one who makes "magic" but also a technician who can learn the "secrets" of the trade, an artisan with "techniques and execution" that distinguish her from her counterparts whose "unruly and undisciplined" students essentially run wild in the classroom. (Yes, it is interesting to see the power of images in Lemov's view of students, too.)

Like Lemov, I refuse to think that only a few teachers can achieve excellence. Having taught actors and teachers now for over thirty years, I believe these practices can be taught, but I am also extremely humble about the challenges I've faced as a teacher and my students have faced as learners. And there are so many other challenges, as well, such as how to truly listen and be present to all of the emotional and cognitive complexities being felt and experienced in the space. (This, by the way, is another dimension on which the work of theatre artists and teachers are analogous—both have to master the art of listening and the challenge of being fully present in the moment.)

While a full exploration of the differences and relationship between craft and art are far beyond my capacity (I won't even claim the problem of limited space!), I want to suggest one distinction that I believe supports my argument that both craft and artistry are required of teachers and also supports my belief that the premises of this book are fundamental to the improvement of teaching. I want to start, though, by emphasizing that I don't see craft and artistry as dichotomized or in opposition, despite prevailing popular sentiment that they are both. But then I don't see an essential dichotomy between objectivity and subjectivity. Indeed, I believe that it is in the mix and negotiation of those perspectives that we discover the deepest human truths (in art, for example) and that we develop our most profound understandings of the phenomena of this world (in our academic studies, as well as in professional endeavors).

In this context, then, I see craft as having a strongly objective dimension with agreed-upon standards of quality and how those standards are most commonly and effectively achieved in a particular domain. What are the characteristics of a well-made shoe, shovel, or sushi? And how best to achieve those dimensions of quality? These are the tricks of the trade, the craftsperson's knowledge and skill, handed down and refined from one generation to the next. In this way, craft comprises a set of established truths of a particular field of practice. Of course, these established truths shift, change, and evolve, but that's both the nature of truths and of craft. These evolutions, I believe, are the result of negotiations between new and subjective perspectives and those more objective knowledges held in the collective wisdom of the community of craftspeople.

So when, then, does artistry enter the picture? I would argue that this is at the moment when the subjective is called for and engaged. In every creative act there are choices to make. It could be done this way or that way, so which would be better—which is the best choice or solution given these materials, this specific purpose, this moment in history, this audience or user? At that moment, the craftsperson enters the subjective realm and, I would argue, the realm of artistry.

It is in this way, or at this same moment, that teaching must move beyond craft to artistry, not as a matter of putting one's stamp on the lesson, but because context counts and the moment matters. The history of success or failure your students have experienced in school counts as you decide how to introduce an assignment. The condition of the school building makes a difference to every lesson taught within its walls. The spirit and culture of the school support or undermine the learning experience.

It matters what the students in front of you find deeply interesting and/or confusing (often the same things) or what has been happening in the world (think of the murders in Newtown, Connecticut, or the reelection of the first African American president of the United States) or the joys and discoveries students have made during out-of-school hours (inspired by family members, organized activities, or adventures of many kinds with friends). It matters what happened to your students in the class before the one you are teaching right now. Again, context counts and the moment matters.

There are many techniques and tried-and-true solutions that one learns on the path to becoming a master teacher; these are all part of the craft of teaching. But when do we learn (and who teaches us) which one to use at a particular moment and when to abandon all of the known techniques and solutions and invent something new in the moment? That's when subjectivity, if trusted, is called for and, if supplied, can be the difference that makes all the difference. And that is artistry.

And that is what this book aims toward: the creation, within the all-too-often inhospitable realm of schools, of spaces for "collective creation" and the encouragement of artistry in teaching. Not the artistry of an inspired individual, but the intentional collective artistry of teachers who work as hard outside the classroom as they do inside it to prepare themselves for the moments of improvisation and invention that all teaching requires. It is precisely in this book's vision of the collective nature of this work that the individual perspectives and instincts of these teachers are examined and negotiated and that intersubjective insights are achieved. This is the way craft changes over a long time.

Many will read this book, shake their heads, and sigh, sadly concluding that this vision is lovely but unrealistic. Teachers aren't artists and any comparison immediately sets effective teaching outside the reach of the vast majority of teachers. I return to my first "move," from images to realities, and suggest that it depends on your image of the teacher, the student, and the school. And, again, be careful what you imagine—it will likely become the reality.

I also return to my early suggestion that this is a radical book. It is, befitting the author's character, quietly radical. It doesn't create battle scenarios and sound trumpets. It doesn't claim to be *the* solution to education's ills. It is much more radical than that. David Allen offers us an image of teachers that is exponentially richer and more hopeful than almost any image actively in use in contemporary educational discourse. In exceptionally clear and specific terms, this book embraces the artistry essential to the craft of teaching and shows a path forward toward that uncompromising vision.

Preface

To begin, a disclosure and a declaration: I am a teacher educator, researcher, and facilitator of learning groups for teachers and school administrators—definitely not an actor or director or, for that matter, a trained scholar of the performing arts. As a committed dilettante, however, I believe that great theatre-going experiences can affect how we see and think about experiences in our everyday, nontheatrical lives.

As an educator, I believe that understanding how theatre artists collaborate to develop new work can inform how teachers collaborate to create knowledge about student learning, as well as instructional strategies and tools to support it. I open with the story of my own experiences with theatre because it is the story of how these beliefs came to be.

Before my junior year of college, I didn't think about theatre much, if at all. I had seen precisely one professionally performed play, during a high school trip to New York City, a rather puzzling (to me) production of *Betrayal* by Harold Pinter. That changed quickly and irrevocably during the three months I spent in London on a semester abroad program dedicated to British literature and Shakespeare. We saw two or three plays a week—from a one-man performance in a tiny space above a pub to debuts in old West End theatres to main stage productions of the Royal Shakespeare Company and the National Theatre.

When we weren't seeing plays, we were reading them, acting out scenes from them, and tirelessly talking about them. While I have never achieved the same frequency of theatre-going, I have been seeing plays ever since—I've found that an educator's salary only encourages my interest in experimental or Off-Off-Broadway productions.

Like many people who love theatre, I have become interested in the ways plays are developed, from playwriting to rehearsal to performance. At several points in my life, I've had—or contrived to have—the opportunity to indulge this interest up close. The first came during that semester in London in meetings our group had with Royal Shakespeare Company actors. In these discussions, we learned about some of the decisions actors and directors make, as well as the range of professional and personal experiences they draw upon in constructing their characters.

About ten years later, I was teaching English in Warsaw. With a tenuous grasp of the language, I started to explore the rich Polish theatre scene. My tutor, Kasia, a former theatre student at the university, suggested a trip to the famed Gardzienice Centre for Theatre Practices, located in a remote village outside Lublin. We saw two dark and beautiful performances. My most vivid memory of the trip, though, is of squeezing into the converted stable the company used as a rehearsal space and small theatre to observe the director, Wlodzimierz Staniewski, working with the actors.

Staniewski led the actors through a series of strenuous physical exercises and then a rehearsal of one of the scenes from a play the company would perform that evening. I was amazed by how the actors and director discovered new details in their verbal expressions and movements in a production long part of the company's repertoire, for example, the exquisite tenderness with which an actress brings a loaf of peasant bread to her breast.

Fast-forward another fifteen years: I am sitting in a "black box" theatre space at Columbia University, observing the Collaboration class taught by Anne Bogart, director of Columbia's graduate directing program and co-founder of the SITI Company. The student actors, writers, and directors are rehearsing original plays they have collaboratively created and will perform as their program theses. I am riveted by the quality of attention with which Bogart observes the performers, as well as the kinds of questions and observations she offers them as notes—asking the performers to "do something stupid" or to reimagine their piece in relation to a Verdi aria (more about this soon).

By this point, my interest in the theatre artists' practices was no longer merely casual. I had spent the last decade facilitating, studying, and writing about teacher inquiry groups in schools. The more I reflected on these groups' work, the more threads I could see connecting their interactions and those of theatre companies like the SITI Company, the Ghost Road Company, Pig Iron Theatre Company, Complicite, and others whose methods for creating new work are fundamentally collaborative.

Several years earlier, along with Steve Seidel, my colleague from Harvard Project Zero, I had taken part in a conference sponsored by the Chicago Arts Partnerships in Education, in which we'd demonstrated methods used by teachers for collaborative reflection on students' work and their instructional practice. At the same conference, the choreographer Liz Lerman facilitated her Critical Response Process by reflecting on a local dance company's performance (see chapter 6). Clearly, others were also finding the dialogue across the domains compelling.

These connections resisted facile comparisons: teacher as actor, classroom as stage, and so on; rather they opened what the philosopher Maxine Greene (1995) calls a "conceptual space" to explore questions about practice in the two domains. Foremost among these, and the question that inspired this book, is how educators can learn from theatre artists about our own collaborative practices and how our practices support teachers' professional learning and instructional improvement.

This book is for teachers and teacher educators who, like me, believe that inquiry groups, study groups, critical friends groups, and other teacher learning groups offer the most powerful form of professional learning and the engine for instructional improvement. As we are committed to collaborative learning practices, we must also recognize that these groups' work often falls short of their promise, both in terms of the groups' depth of reflective discussion and impact on teachers' instructional practices.

There are many ways to reflect critically on the work of teacher learning groups that could lead to richer professional learning and instructional improvement. In this book I explore one that brings together my investigation of theatre arts practices with my study of teachers' professional development in schools.

By doing so, I contribute to a dialogue between arts and education initiated by Dewey (1916) when he declared, "the method of teaching is the method of an art" (p. 170). In doing so, I follow teachers and thinkers including Maxine Greene, Phillip Jackson (1998), Elliot Eisner (2002), and others. I hope my efforts similarly invite others to enter the play of ideas and practices that working across the arts and education entails. It is indeed "serious play," when we consider its implications for deepening the professional learning of teachers and improving the learning experiences of their students.

Acknowledgments

The author wishes to thank the following individuals for their contributions to the book: Anne Bogart and Leon Ingulsrud of the SITI Company, New York City; Katharine Noon, Christel Joy Johnson, and Brian Weir of the Ghost Road Company, Los Angeles, as well as fellow participants in the company's 2011 Ko Festival workshop; Alexandra Dorer, Carla Meskill, Dorothy S. Pam, and Beth Watkins; and Quinn Bauriedel of the Pig Iron Company, Philadelphia.

Colleagues and friends from Project Zero, the Harvard Graduate School of Education, especially Tina Blythe, Mara Krechevsky, Ron Ritchhart, Melissa Rivard, Steve Seidel, Denise Simon, Terri Turner, Shirley Veenema, and Daniel Gray Wilson.

Teachers and administrators of Park East High School, East Harlem, New York City, especially Drew Allsopp, Peter Lapré, Kevin McCarthy, Clancy McKenna, Suzanne Wichterle Ort, Lisa Purcell, Jennie Reist, Darren Schmidt, Joseph Schmidt, Stuart Smith, J. C. Whittaker, and Carrie Worthington. Teachers and administrators of Fisher Hill Elementary School, Orange, Massachusetts; the Harbor School, Boston; and the Jacob Hiatt Magnet School, Worcester, Massachusetts. Lead teachers and directors from the SEDUC schools in Santiago, Chile. Nicole Chasse and Gina Stefanini from the Edward Devotion School, Brookline, Massachusetts; Debi Milligan from the Cambridge Rindge and Latin School, Cambridge, Massachusetts.

My writing group: Shira Epstein, Elisabeth Johnson, Melissa Shieble, Jason Wirtz, Laura Gellert, and Bill Proefriedt. From Teachers College, Columbia University: John Baldacchino, Thomas Hatch, Victoria Marsick, Ruth Vinz, and Lyle Yorks. And those who helped to put the last pieces of the book together: Donald Freeman, Frances Hensley, Samuel Hammond, Jillian Shafer, Teri Schrader, and Nancy Thorne.

Finally, I'd like to express my gratitude for their encouragement, support, and friendship to Tina Blythe, Markie Hancock, Joe McDonald, Suzanne Wichterle Ort, and Steve Seidel.

Introduction

Thinking with the Theatre Arts

Over the past two decades, the practice of teachers meeting regularly in organized groups within their schools has become increasingly commonplace. Referred to as inquiry groups, critical friends groups, grade-level teams, or professional learning communities (PLCs), these groups are intended to be sites for teachers' professional learning and instructional improvement. As such teacher learning groups (TLGs) become more common, researchers have sought to understand how their practices support and constrain teachers' professional learning—about curriculum, pedagogy, assessment, their content areas, and more—and instructional improvement.

Some researchers have employed theoretical perspectives and analytical tools that posit learning occurs through participation in social interaction rather than through acquisition, that is, by direct transmission from the relatively expert to relatively novice (Rogoff, Baker-Sennett, Lacasa, & Goldsmith, 1995). While these studies have helped us to appreciate important aspects of activity within TLGs, they have only begun to open the "black box of professional community" (Little, 2003) in order to understand how teachers learn together and what makes such learning possible and productive.

A more recent approach to understanding teacher learning is to investigate practices across professional domains. In one influential study, researchers analyzed the preservice preparation of teachers, clinical psychologists, and ministers (Grossman, Compton, Igra, Ronfeldt, Shahan, & Williamson,

2009). Before interning in actual worksites, novice psychologists and ministers benefit from extensive and substantive opportunities for "approximations of practice"; for example, novice ministers prepare and deliver sermons to their instructors and fellow students, then receive detailed feedback. By contrast, in their review of teacher education programs, Grossman and her colleagues found such approximations of practice before student teaching all but absent.

The training of doctors provides another useful site for cross-professional inquiry. To overcome the limits of the single-classroom placements typical of student teaching in many teacher education programs, Moje (2011) proposed that student teachers complete a "rotation" among different school and classroom settings, each with a specific pedagogical focus, much as doctors do in clinical rounds; for instance, in one site, the focus might be inclusion of special needs students into mainstream classes, in another, supporting students' development of literacy skills.

This book extends this cross-domain methodology from teachers' preservice experiences to those of practicing teachers—veterans and relative novices—working together in TLGs within their own schools. It explores the practices of theatre artists whose working methods are fundamentally collaborative. The goals for doing so are: (1) to open up different ways of seeing TLG practices and how they promote (or constrain) opportunities for teachers' learning; (2) to propose new resources for TLGs, such as tools to structure their meetings and foster critical self-reflection on their practices; and (3) to contribute to a dialogue between educators and theatre artists about collaborative practice.

THE ILLUMINATIVE POWER OF THE ARTS

The focus on theatre arts as a source for thinking about teacher learning begs the question, why the arts at all when medicine or social work or even military training might offer more direct analogies to teaching? As is so often the case for educators, John Dewey provides an answer—or perhaps a better idea of the question we are asking. For Dewey (1934), the experience of creating or perceiving a work of art is continuous with—not separate from—experiences from all domains of life, whether parenting, playing soccer, or developing a lesson plan. In fact, by isolating arts-based experiences from others, we sacrifice the potential to transform how we appreciate experiences in other spheres of life and to make them more satisfying (Jackson, 1998).

Through attention to the qualities of "esthetic experiences," Dewey maintains, our perception of the nature of any experience may become clearer and more intense; in other words, we will be able to see, in new light and detail, taken-for-granted qualities and relationships that inhere within any experience, for example, that of a TLG developing a group inquiry question. Not only do the arts serve as a means to reflect on experiences that have come before, they also provide a "platform for seeing things in a way they are not normally seen. In doing so, they help us to wonder, 'Why not?'" (Eisner, 2002, p. 83). Thus, they can help us to reconstruct our practices to be more effective going forward.

Bold claims for the illuminative and imaginative potential of the arts—but how do we actually go about harnessing it? Some scholars have invoked the arts, or a specific form of the arts, as a metaphor for teaching, for example, teaching as storytelling (Egan, 1986) or as a performance art (Sarason, 1999), or the classroom as an artist's studio (Schreck, 2009). While recognizing the "generative power evident in metaphor" (Egan, 1997, p. 55), this book focuses on the specific *practices* of theatre artists. It tries to understand how these practices generate the performances that are a theatre company's products and to relate this understanding to the practices and products of TLGs.

The next section offers a vignette from Anne Bogart's Collaboration course, referred to in the preface, to illustrate how thinking with the theatre arts offers resources for understanding the practices of TLGs. Bogart is one of a growing number of theatre artists who practice "collective creation" (Chen, Pulinkala, & Robinson, 2010), or "devised theatre" (Oddey, 1994), that is the collaborative development of a work for performance, as opposed to the more familiar interpretation of an existing script. These practices, explored in detail in chapter 3, represent a critical and largely untapped conceptual resource for understanding collaborative practices within TLGs and making them more productive of teacher learning and instructional improvement.

Back to Class

In a black box theatre space in the basement of a nondescript building off Broadway, groups of graduate student actors, playwrights, directors, stage managers, and dramaturges are working on their final project for the course. Each group has been creating an original play, including script, lighting, set design, sound design, props, and costumes. During the full-day class meeting, each group will present a scene from its piece in progress. Bogart and the performers' classmates (and sometimes actors from the SITI Company) give notes or feedback to the performing group. In just a few weeks, the groups will perform their completed pieces for an audience in the same space.

The third performance group of the morning performs its scene, an encounter between a young man and young woman, strangers who have survived some kind of apocalyptic event. From where I sit in the last row of bleachers that lines the back wall of the space, I can observe Bogart as well as the (temporarily) nonperforming student actors, directors, and designers. Bogart, sitting in the first row, leans in toward the performers at a nearly 45-degree angle—her characteristic pose in working with her own SITI Company. Her expression communicates a deep attentiveness to all that is going on before her.

As is customary for the class, she stops the action after about twenty minutes for the observers to give notes to the actors, director, and playwright. She begins with a question to the audience: "How are you doing with [the sense of] time passing?" After a few rather general comments from fellow actors and directors, she shares her own observations: "[There is a] really strong pull through the scene. [But] the actors are losing energy in transitions. Do something stupid," she suggests, adding, "in a good sense." The theatre students recognize Bogart's shorthand for inserting something new and specific—a movement, use of lighting, a prop, and so on—into the scene as a way to change the dynamic and open up new possibilities for development.

"Treat the opening [of the scene] like an aria—listen to Verdi," Bogart advises. "[It] can be more *differentiated.*" To illustrate the quality of differentiation, she offers a second reference: "Did you ever see Fassbinder's *Bitter Tears of Petra von Kant*? Hanna Schygulla spends 20 minutes waiting for a call. *Mine it.* There is a series of things you go through when you're waiting."

As she concludes her notes, she asks the performers, "How are you guys doing?" Then, before the class breaks for lunch, she turns and scans the audience: "Everybody okay?"

What the Vignette Reveals

This tiny slice from the class illustrates some of the elements that contribute to the creation of a play—elements with useful analogues to practices of TLGs.

One element is the attentiveness demonstrated by Anne Bogart in how she leans forward into the action in the scene playing out before her. For Dewey (1934), the development of any work of art over time depends less upon inspiration than on "continuity of attention and endurance." Bogart's attention to the performers, which she simultaneously enacts and models for her students, embodies Dewey's "power of continuous attention" (p. 137), without which, the kinds of specific questions and comments she offers to the actors would be impossible.

Another element is the variety of resources, or materials, employed in developing a scene or play. These extend far beyond what is in the script; for instance, Bogart offers the actors the comparison of the sense of time passing they are creating to a Verdi aria and to the image of an actress waiting for the phone to ring in a particular scene from a Fassbinder film.

Thus, a visual image or musical reference can serve as a resource for the actors—one just as real and applicable to the developing work as new line of text or the introduction of a new prop. The extraordinary attention artists devote to the materials of collective creation is evident in Bogart's encouragement of the actors to "mine" individual moments in the scene even as they strive for an overall coherence of tone and feeling.

The structure for creating a work is another important element of collective creation. Here, Bogart facilitates the provision of feedback on the work in process. What we do not see are the prior exercises the groups have engaged in to initiate and develop the pieces. Bogart and her collaborator Tina Landau (2005) use a method they call Composition to structure the process of collective creation, from identifying questions to address, to gathering materials and exploring possibilities, to composing, performing, and reflecting on pieces. The ultimate product, the play as performed, integrates a series of earlier products generated collectively through these early steps.

Composition and other methods for collective creation illustrate the "cumulative progression" Dewey (1934) equated with creating a work of art, a continual ordering and reordering of the "meanings" that have been discovered through the artists' thoughts and actions. For Dewey and the theatre artists who engage in collective creation, the process depends, almost paradoxically, on *not knowing* the shape and dimensions of the ultimate product. A predetermined product kills creation.

For theatre artists that product is, of course, a performance of some kind (a play, dance, etc.). But what about the products of TLGs' activity? And how do they relate to the professional learning and instructional improvement for which the groups exist in the first place?

TEACHER LEARNING AS PERFORMANCE

How do we know what teachers collaborating with colleagues in an inquiry group, study group, or grade-level team are learning? Of course, we could survey teachers, conduct interviews, perhaps even construct evaluations of some kind. What really matters, though, is what the teachers do with their learning, both in their classrooms and in their work with colleagues. In other words, we look for understanding in how it is *performed*—much the way we look for what actors have learned about the play (its themes, the story, their own characters, relationships among characters, and so on) in what they perform for an audience.

Of course, the "performances of understanding" (Perkins & Blythe, 1994) that theatre companies give are qualitatively different than the ones teachers give. But both depend on creating products that can be performed, that is, that can be applied in different settings (on stage or in a rehearsal studio; in the classroom or in a professional development session) and that make the group's learning available for reflection, refinement, and revision.

This is what the teachers of the preschools of Reggio Emilia, Italy, mean when they speak of "making learning visible." There, visual arts provides a critical metaphor (the "atelier," or studio) and set of practices (Project Zero & Reggio Children, 2001). In a similar fashion, this book draws metaphors and practices from theatre arts.

In fact, we already talk about a teacher's job *performance*. But we don't tend to talk about specific *performances* that teachers create and perform *with* their students and their colleagues. And when we do talk about a teacher's performance, we generally talk about it as an individual performance rather than one that is the product of a group. For theatre artists, though, an individual actor's performance—even if alone on stage—is understood to be the product of the ensemble that developed it.

But theatre artists create and perform plays and dances. What do TLGs create and perform? Throughout this book, two categories of products-as-performances of TLGs are highlighted: instructional resources and conceptual resources.

Instructional resources are those that can be applied (with adaptation) within the classroom; they include strategies (e.g., for supporting students' writing or problem-solving); student tasks (e.g., assignments, projects, activities); assessment instruments (e.g., rubrics); and many others. Conceptual resources give form to teacher learning about instruction and student learning. They include inquiry questions, frameworks and analytical categories for discussing student learning, visual representations (e.g., concept maps), metaphors (e.g., "classroom as studio"), and many others.

These categories are not sealed; there is always potential for movement among them. For example, conceptual frameworks for analyzing student writing may influence the creation and use of specific rubrics to assess students' writing; a strategy for modeling problem-solving that has been used with students can become the basis for an inquiry question about stages of problem-solving. This fluidity suggests that process and product are not separate but continuous, as they are in a work of art (Dewey, 1934).

Like the Composition exercises, improvisations, and rehearsals actors engage in during the development of a production, the instructional strategies, inquiry questions, and other instructional and conceptual resources teachers create and use are *works in process*, and as such, are open to critical reflection and reconstruction. To obtain these goals for TLGs, it serves to look closely at key dimensions of how theatre artists create their performances-as-products.

A FRAMEWORK FOR COLLECTIVE CREATION: MEANS, MATERIALS, MODES

Returning to the vignette from the Collaboration class, it is possible to identify three dimensions that contribute to the theatre artists' creation of performances. These three dimensions—means, materials, and modes of engagement—comprise the analytical model used throughout the book to investigate activity in TLGs and propose resources to enhance the groups' effectiveness (see figure I.1).

The term *means* designates the structures and tools groups employ to initiate and guide their processes of collective creation. The vignette from Bogart's Collaboration class offered just one moment from one group's work; this mo-

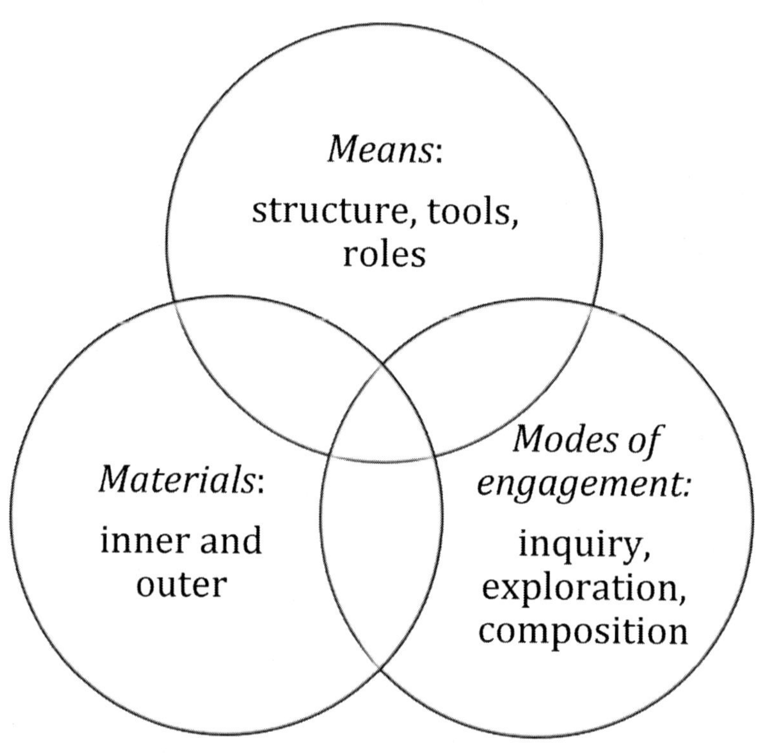

FIGURE I.1
Model for collective creation.

ment exists within a longer process that structures the work of the groups in the class, from identifying questions to initiate the process to gathering materials through performing the finished piece. Similarly, TLGs often use inquiry cycles to sequence and focus their work over time, typically beginning with the framing of inquiry questions and specifying some of the ways the group will productively explore the questions.

Theatre artists employ specific tools at specific points in their processes, for example, exercises generate new possibilities that may contribute to the development of the ultimate performance. Similarly, TLGs commonly use protocols to structure discussions and analyses of participants' instruction and their students' learning (McDonald, Mohr, Dichter, & McDonald, 2007).

Means also refers to specific roles participants play within the group, especially the director in a theatre company and the facilitator in a TLG. Participants playing these roles enact specific skills and dispositions that contribute to the group's productive use of structures and tools (Allen & Blythe, 2004), a topic for chapter 6.

Participants in collaborative groups bring all kinds of resources to the table (or the studio floor); these represent the materials through which they create new work. For theatre artists, these *materials* include the script (if there is one) but also information gleaned from research, or "source work" (Bogart & Landau, 2005), which the director and actors might conduct about the characters, the setting, the period, and so on. For TLGs, materials might include samples of their students' work; the tasks, scoring rubrics, and other resources teachers create; texts of all kinds; curriculum standards; data on student achievement; research on effective practices; and many others.

These constitute, for Dewey (1934), *outer* materials, that is, the physical artifacts one can pick up, examine, and point to; for Dewey, no less real or vital are the *inner* materials participants engage with in perceiving or creating an art work: "images, observations, memories, and emotions" (p. 77). Just as the image Bogart offers of the actress waiting for the phone in the film might be materially important to the actors working on the scene, so might a teacher's image of her students at work on a math problem—or even memories of her own experiences as a student—be materially important to her TLG's collective learning and, ultimately, instructional improvement.

Modes of engagement highlights the dispositions that contribute to the group working collaboratively and productively. It describes the orientation of participants in the group to one another and to their collective activity at any given point in time. In theatre arts companies that are engaged in collective creation, a dominant mode is inquiry into a question or problem that initiates and motivates the process of creation.

Inquiry is complemented by a mode of "lateral thinking" (de Bono, 1990), in which the company freely explores ideas and possibilities related to the question. Later, a group's mode will shift to composing new possibilities for performance and reflecting on these.

For TLGs engaging in collective creation, modes of inquiry, exploration, and composition replace more familiar modes of problem-solving or validation of existing practices.

COMPOSING THE BOOK

Readers may be relieved to know that the book does not propose teachers put on blindfolds and spar with newspaper swords or take part in other theatre arts games—valuable though they might be for other purposes (see appendix for resources for these). The goal here is not to turn teachers into actors or directors, mimicking theatre arts practices or exercises. Instead, it is to challenge educators to view their own (sometimes taken for granted) collaborative learning practices anew and reflect on how they serve our purposes—much like seeing great theatre can encourage us to view our lives through new eyes.

The sources for the book include my studies of TLGs, as well as those conducted by other researchers, my experiences facilitating TLGs in different school settings, and research on professional learning communities, teacher inquiry groups, and other forms of teacher learning.

On the theatre arts side, sources include observations of theatre artists at work, interviews with actors and directors, especially those practicing methods for collective creation, and my participation in workshops offered by the Ghost Road Company (Los Angeles) and the Pig Iron Theatre Company (Philadelphia). Other data include "talkbacks" with playwrights and actors after a performance, interviews with and profiles of theatre artists, theatre artists' accounts of their own practices, and scholarship in dramaturgical practice and collaborative creativity.

If these provide the materials for the book, the means involves moving continually between the domains of theatre arts and teacher learning in groups, mining practices from each and exploring relationships among them. The mode of engagement aspires to the "aesthetic attitude" Nelson Goodman (1972) described as "restless, searching, testing" (p. 103)—a mode that characterizes the work of theatre arts companies and TLGs that I admire.

Outline of the Chapters

The structure of the book reflects this dialogic and exploratory approach. Chapter 1 describes the features and functions of TLGs, including inquiry groups, study groups, critical friends groups, and other configurations. It relates these groups' practices to the hallmarks of professional learning communities within schools: collaboration, reflective dialogue on practice, and collective responsibility for students' and colleagues' learning (Hord, 1997;

Grossman, Wineburg, & Woolworth, 2001; Louis, Kruse, & Marks, 1996; Stevens & Kahne, 2006).

It also considers critiques of TLGs' practices and outcomes, from a "contrived collegiality" (Hargreaves & Dawe, 1990; Hargreaves & Fullan, 2012), which serves administrative functions at the cost of teachers' autonomy, to tunnel vision on test-score data (Louis, 2008), to "shallowness" of professional dialogue (Curry, 2008), to an absence of focus on pedagogical content knowledge (Bausmth & Barry, 2011). These critiques invite new ways of both analyzing and organizing the work of TLGs.

Chapter 2 provides a brief history of the use of theatre arts metaphors and practices in relation to teaching and teacher learning, from teaching as a performance art (Sarason, 1999) to teacher learning as "coached rehearsal" (Lewis, 2011; Scott, 2008). While some of these are constrained by either a tight focus on the individual teacher or a limited appreciation of theatre arts practices, others demonstrate the potential for a richer dialogue across the domains of theatre and teacher learning in groups—a potential this book exploits.

Chapter 3 investigates specific theatre arts practices that offer resources for reviewing activity within TLGs. In particular, it focuses on the methods of Anne Bogart and her collaborator Tina Landau, introduced earlier; the RSVP Cycles developed by Lawrence and Anna Halprin; and the work of the Ghost Road Company and the Pig Iron Company, in whose workshops I participated. It draws on these and other theatre artists' practices, as well as theoretical perspectives from the arts, collaborative creativity theory, and situated learning theory to elaborate the framework for collective creativity—means, materials, modes of engagement—introduced above.

In chapter 4, the primary focus shifts back to TLGs, now strongly informed by thinking with the theatre arts. It offers a case study of an elementary school TLG in its first two years working together. The framework for collective creation is used to investigate how the group's activity at different points in its history contributes to or constrains the composition of resources for instructional improvement and for the teachers' professional learning.

Chapter 5 investigates an important temporal dimension of collective creation. It begins with a consideration of how theatre artists exploit both short-term episodes of "Exquisite Pressure" (Bogart, 2001), with its deliberately applied constraints of time and materials, and longer-term "cumulative progression" (Dewey, 1934) that integrates and advances experiences and products developed over time (months or even years). It demonstrates how the two timescales function within the collective creation of teachers working with an instructional coach in a small New York City public high school.

Chapter 6 considers the means for initiating or deepening collective creation within schools. It focuses on two essential conditions: a process for collective creation and direction of the process. For the first, it shares examples and resources from TLGs and projects that support them. For the second, it proposes ways of thinking about the responsibilities of coach, facilitator, or lead teacher within TLGs that reflect those of the director in collective creation in theatre arts: making process, not controlling the product.

The concluding chapter offers three "cues" for action for educators committed to professional learning community: begin with listening, give attention, and emphasize rigorous creation. These lessons from theatre companies provide starting points to reinvigorate teacher learning practice so that it is more powerful—and satisfying—for teachers and more generative of instruction that supports their students' learning. The appendix that follows provides references to more resources to put collective creation to work in TLGs and schools.

1

Teacher Learning Groups

Practices, Problems, and Possibilities

In an elementary school in Massachusetts, a group of five teachers, grades four to six, meet twice a month to investigate questions about teaching and student learning, including "How can I help my students become better at self-editing?" and "Do I talk too much?" Between meetings, the teachers gather samples of student work and other artifacts from their classrooms related to their questions. During the meetings, they focus on one teacher's question at a time, using a discussion protocol to reflect on the artifacts, or "evidence," presented and the implications for classroom instruction.

~

Social studies teachers at a small public high school in East Harlem meet with their school's instructional coach to discuss how a first-year teacher might use film with her ninth-grade class. She proposes having each student choose a film with "political content" as an independent project. A more experienced teacher describes strategies he and a colleague have used in their humanities class to "teach students how to watch a film" for plot, setting, and so on.

~

Teacher leaders from five independent schools in Santiago, Chile, meet monthly to discuss their experiences facilitating study groups in their own schools. One teacher leader talks about the "thinking routines" teachers in her group have tried in their classes, for example, "See-Think-Wonder" (Ritchhart, Church, & Morrison, 2011), in which students respond to a new text or image by first describing what they see, then talking about what they think about it, and finally generating questions about it.

~

Three groups working in very different contexts, each with a unique composition of teachers and a unique focus for their meetings. What they have in common is that they are striving to expand and deepen participants' knowledge about instruction. And, in each case, knowledge about instruction is linked to improving students' learning. Each of these groups is an example of a teacher learning group, or TLG for short—key vehicles for developing schoolwide professional community.

The teachers in the Massachusetts elementary school are exploring explicit questions they have identified about how to scaffold their students' writing development through their writing assignments, instructions to students, and teacher modeling. Their meetings explore critical tensions related to teaching writing, including how teachers can help their students to both succeed on the state tests and to develop writing skills for the myriad purposes and audiences the tests don't address.

The teachers in the East Harlem social studies department might be surprised to find themselves described as a learning group at all. On one level, they're doing what teachers have always done, helping a colleague with a very immediate problem, in this case, how to use film effectively as an instructional resource. At the same time, they are supporting each other's knowledge about and skills in developing curriculum and instructional planning. Here, an implicit question or problem focuses their discussion: how do we identify resources and integrate them into our teaching to meet our learning goals for students?

The teacher leaders in Santiago are not focused on their own students' learning in their monthly meetings, not directly, anyway. Instead, they are exploring the problems and possibilities of facilitating the learning of their colleagues back in their own schools. Their discussions investigate such problems as structuring their groups' meetings to focus on students' understandings and involving all teachers actively in the group's discussions.

As these examples suggest, TLGs take many forms. They also go by many different names: professional learning communities, inquiry groups, critical friends groups, study groups, teacher research groups, and others. These names denote different emphases; for example, a critical friends group might focus on providing feedback on one of the teachers' student inquiry project; a teacher research group might investigate a problem the group has identified related to instruction or student learning; a study group might review published research on a new instructional strategy. What unites these forms is that all these seek to build participants' knowledge about student learning, instruction, curriculum development, subject matter content, and skills—essential ingredients of teaching and learning.

This chapter examines the work of TLGs as a precursor to exploring what a theatre arts–based lens reveals about the groups' activitites and how they might be strengthened. It begins by relating TLGs to the emergence of professional learning community as a formulation for teachers' in-service professional development. A more extended vignette from the elementary school in Massachusetts introduced above follows, used here to highlight common features of TLGs' activities. The chapter concludes with a consideration of the benefits of TLGs and some of the recent critiques of their effectiveness—critiques that invite new ways of thinking about and supporting TLGS' work.

TLGS AND PROFESSIONAL LEARNING COMMUNITY

Over the last two decades or so, the professional development of teachers has undergone a sea change. Rather than developing their professional knowledge and skills through workshops, institutes, and courses outside the school, teachers do so with colleagues within the schools in which they actually teach (McLaughlin & Talbert, 2001; Wood, 2007). Schools thus become institutions not only for students' learning but for teachers' as well, in other words, professional learning communities.

The model of schoolwide professional learning community highlights these features: (1) high levels of collaboration among the teachers; (2) ongoing reflective dialogue, or inquiry, about instructional practices and student learning; and (3) collective responsibility for student and teacher learning (Hord, 1997; Grossman, Wineburg, & Woolworth, 2001; Little, 2007; Stevens

& Kahne, 2006). These features dovetail with emerging evidence that professional community is a key factor determining a school's success in supporting student learning, along with leadership, instructional coherence, family/community–school ties, and a student-centered learning climate (Bryk, Sebring, Allensworth, Luppescu, & Easton, 2010).

To realize the goal of professional learning community, teachers work together in groups that meet regularly, which might be designated as inquiry groups, teacher research groups, or "PLCs." More traditional configurations such as grade-level teams and disciplinary departments also serve as vehicles for a schoolwide professional learning community, provided their practices model collaboration, reflection on practice, and mutual responsibility for professional learning and the learning of all students.

INSIDE TLGS

This section presents a TLG meeting from Cooper Elementary School[1] as an image of what goes on in TLG meetings. Of course, meetings of different groups in different contexts will have their own unique activities and characteristics. Nevertheless, this example offers a touchstone for the elements that are common to many TLG meetings, through which the groups strive to advance their professional learning and formulate instructional improvement. (The group's activity is described in greater detail in chapter 4.)

A Teacher Learning Group Meeting

March 23, 9:05 a.m. Five teachers gather in the school's teacher resource room for one of their twice-monthly inquiry group meetings (the second meeting a month is held after school). The group includes teachers from both the mainstream and the two-way bilingual (English-Spanish) programs. The teachers meet, with a break, for the next two hours; occasionally another teacher enters to use the photocopier, exchange greetings, or ask a question, or the public address system barks out an announcement.

As usual, there are donuts and juice on the table along with the manila folders and samples of student work the teachers have brought to the meeting. After a few minutes of catching up, Nora, a fifth-grade teacher and the group's designated facilitator, begins the meeting proper by telling the group about a technology-based research workshop she attended at another school in the district. Devin, another fifth-grade teacher, teases her about how much she must have missed being with her students. Nora laughs and moves the group to its agenda for the meeting. The group plans to do three "mini protocols," as they call the tool for the discussion of the presenting teacher's inquiry question and the artifacts, or evidence, from the classroom to explore it.

Nora facilitates the first protocol, which focuses on Devin's inquiry question: "How can I use students' writers notebooks to support their writing?" Nora asks Devin to describe the evidence he has brought from his classroom and talk about what it tells him about his inquiry question. Devin briefly describes the three samples of writing he has brought, all by one student, Marta: an essay based on the reading "Trapped in Tar," a research paper, and a short piece written very early in the school year.

Devin talks about the changes in his students' writing, especially in how students "use personal experience in writing," pointing to some examples in Marta's work. Nevertheless, he tells the group, he struggles to "keep the momentum [of his class] on the writer's journal," an instructional approach the teachers had agreed upon at the beginning of the year.

In keeping with the protocol, Nora invites the other teachers in the group to look at the evidence and offer their own comments on what it "says to them" about Devin's question. The teachers point out different types of writing demonstrated in Marta's pieces. For some, the evidence suggests Devin's students may actually be doing what he intended they do in their writer's journals, only in other formats, for example, in their responses to his essay and research assignments.

After a few minutes of conversation, Nora asks Devin if he would like to respond to the group's discussions. Devin tells his colleagues he is pleased that they've also seen evidence for a range of writing. He wonders whether his inquiry question about the writer's journal is the right one for him and whether he might instead explore a question about how he's teaching reading. This leads to a few moments' discussion about differences in using "reading books and basal readers."

All told, the discussion of Devin's questions and the samples of student writing has taken about twenty-five minutes. In the remainder of the meeting, two more teachers present evidence related to their inquiry questions using the same protocol, in one, looking at students' "prewrites" and final essays; in the other, examining two students' math journals and social studies question sheets. Now in their second year as a group and more comfortable with the protocols, the teachers rotate the role of facilitator. The meeting ends at a few minutes past 11:00, not before Nora asks teachers to think about who would like to present evidence in the next meeting in two weeks.

Hallmarks of Teacher Learning Groups' Activitities

Despite diverse configurations and contexts, TLGs share a number of common elements evident in the sample meeting above, in particular: (1) a focusing question or problem; (2) use of artifacts of teaching and learning from classrooms; (3) structures and tools to guide and support the group's activity; and (4) facilitation.

Groups' activities are often driven by questions or problems related to the teachers' own day-to-day classroom practices and their students' learning—usually identified by the participants themselves. This contrasts with more traditional forms of professional development in which the teachers largely follow somebody else's agenda, purposes, and foci.

In the meeting above, the group's discussion is focused by the *questions* Devin and his colleagues have identified early in the school year. In this case, they have also identified a common "umbrella question," uniting their individual questions, about supporting students' writing across the curriculum. In some groups, such an inquiry stance (Cochran-Smith & Lytle, 2009) is acknowledged explicitly. Others may not identify themselves as an inquiry group but the investigation of questions and problems is similarly central to the groups' activities.

Another key aspect of TLGs' practice is to use *artifacts*, or evidence, from teachers' classrooms to address the questions and problems identified by the group. One common source of evidence is the results of standardized tests. Under the banner of greater accountability, schools and teachers are increasingly pressured to use these data in making curricular or instructional decisions of all kinds. However, test results represent just one form of evidence TLGs use—and often the least revealing about student learning (Koretz, 2009).

The more revealing "data of practice" (Cochran-Smith & Lytle, 2009) TLGs reflect on include samples of the students' work—such as the essays, research papers, math journals, and other pieces in the meeting above—as well as observations made about students at work, students' own reflections on their work, audio and video records of classroom interactions, notes from peer observations, and many other forms. Even the stories teachers tell about classroom events provide a potentially valuable form of "anecdotal data" (Nelson, Slavit, & Deuel, 2012) for their investigation. In figure 1.1, teachers in a "Making Learning Visible" project seminar reflect on student work samples and other documentation from a high school photography project (see chapter 6).

Collecting piles of data does not automatically lead to learning. TLGs use *tools* of different kinds to structure and support their activity. Inquiry cycles are a commonly used structure to help groups to organize and sequence how they will use their time over multiple meetings. An exemplary inquiry cycle, like the one created by the Coalition of Essential Schools in figure 1.2, specifies steps for collecting data, analyzing or reflecting on data, and formulating changes in instruction based on the analysis.

Inquiry cycles, while useful as guides, don't determine the pace or even the order of a group's process. Instead, groups monitor and reflect on their own progress and identify the next steps that will be most useful to them—even if that means scrapping or radically revising a question they started out with.

Discussion protocols are an increasingly common tool TLGs use to structure and sequence their work over time, though in much more concentrated

FIGURE 1.1
Reflecting on the "data of practice." Making Learning Visible Project, Project Zero, Harvard Graduate School of Education. Photo by Melissa Rivard.

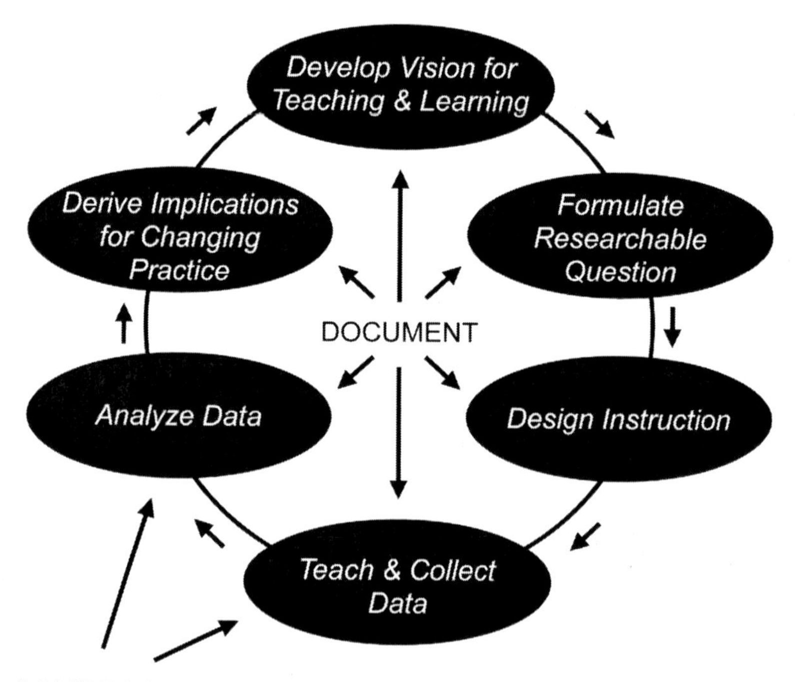

FIGURE 1.2
Cycle of Inquiry and Action. Coalition of Essential Schools, www.essentialschools.org.

periods, a single meeting or segment of a meeting. Protocols typically specify a set of steps for the group's discussion. The group in the meeting above is using the Considering Evidence Protocol, which they nicknamed the "mini protocol," the purpose of which is to encourage different perspectives on what the evidence (artifacts from the classroom) presented indicates about the presenting teacher's question, including implications for additional evidence the presenter might collect or changes in the inquiry question itself. The steps of this protocol are:

1. Presenter reminds group of his/her inquiry question and briefly describes evidence.

2. Presenter reflects on what evidence may tell him/her about the inquiry question.
3. Full group (including presenter) reflects on what evidence may tell them about the inquiry question (Evidence Project Staff, 2001).

Other protocols, usually with a greater number of steps, serve other purposes, for example, providing feedback on a task or instructional strategy, analyzing students' performance in relation to specified learning goals, or uncovering aspects of a student's understanding (McDonald, Mohr, Dichter, & McDonald, 2007).

Not all TLG activities employ discussion protocols. For example, teachers in a group might use a rubric to analyze student performance on a common assessment task. Or they might discuss research on teaching and learning presented in a journal article. Many groups devote time to co-planning curriculum or instruction. And some TLGs engage participants in observing one another teach, offering feedback, and collectively reflecting on their observations.

Whether groups use explicit protocols or not, for TLGs to be effective in supporting teacher learning and instructional improvement requires *facilitation*. TLGs typically have a designated facilitator for their meetings. The facilitator is often a teacher participating in the group, like Nora in the vignette above; in other groups, a coach, staff developer, or administrator facilitates. Whoever plays the role, facilitation calls for specific skills and dispositions beyond simply timekeeping, which can be developed through professional development, observation, and self-reflection (Allen & Blythe, 2004), a subject explored in chapter 6.

This discussion of inquiry cycles, protocols, rubrics, and facilitation may make the work of TLGs sound highly technical and organized, and, to a degree, it is. Like doctors or social workers—or theatre artists—teachers in TLGs have specific ways of interacting with colleagues to identify and solve problems, share knowledge, and develop skills. Sitting in with a TLG, though, quickly reveals the social dimension of their work. Discussions are characterized by joking, storytelling, offering encouragement, and, at times, blowing off steam about the various pressures and challenges of their work. In the group above, Devin's sense of humor, in particular, helps to keep a light tone, even as the group explores vexing questions.

From the standpoint of collective creation in this book, the purpose of using structures and tools is not to make sure these natural social activities don't interfere with the serious work of investigating and improving teaching and learning, but to mine stories, emotions, images, and other representations of experience they provide. As the work of theatre artists reveals, it is the engagement with materials of many kinds—from the concrete to the representational to the emotional—that contributes to the creation of products that are meaningful, satisfying, and useful.

WHY TLGS?

The prominence of TLGs, like the one depicted above, begs the question, why should teachers work together in groups? This section considers both the benefits of TLGs—for teachers and students—and then some of the critiques of their effectiveness. It begins with a few words about how TLGs have come to be so common in the first place.

That teachers in the United States don't spend nearly as much time working with their colleagues as teachers in other developed nations (Darling-Hammond, 2010) does not mean that they don't like working together. Professional norms and school organizational structures have contributed to the "persistence of privacy" endemic in schools, that is, a resistance to exposing one's teaching and students' learning to colleagues (Little, 1982, 1990). One result is that teachers often have little experience with forms of collegial critique and reflection that are common in other professions.

The absence of collaborative professional development in schools also reflects a professional history that framed teaching as largely technical rather than intellectual work. The argument went roughly like this: once you were trained as a teacher in those basic skills required to deliver predetermined curriculum content to students, there was little need for additional professional development (Lagemann, 2000). The in-service professional development teachers did receive, for example, in learning about a new curriculum or instructional strategy, was delivered by so-called experts during "one-shot" trainings or workshops.

As the last century waned, practitioners and researchers challenged the effectiveness of this prevailing model for professional development. For teachers' professional learning and skill development to be effective, they argued, it needed to be ongoing and grounded in the daily work of teachers within their own schools (Ball & Cohen, 1999; McLaughlin & Talbert, 2001). In the intervening years, more and more teachers have begun to interact regularly with colleagues, in TLGs of one stripe or another, as a primary form of their professional development.

Such opportunities are still far too limited. In the 2010 *MetLife Survey of the American Teacher*, including over a thousand public school teachers from across the country, teachers reported, on average, spending just 2.7 hours per week in "structured collaboration" with colleagues—in other words, slightly more than 30 minutes a school day (p. 9). By contrast, teachers in European and Asian countries spend 15 to 20 hours a week engaged in tasks related to teaching, many of which include collaborating with colleagues, such as preparing and reflecting on lessons, developing common assessments and analyzing results, and observing and providing feedback on one another's classrooms (Wei, Darling-Hammond, Andree, Richardson, Orphanos, 2009).

The survey points to clear benefits for teachers and students in schools where collaboration is more prevalent. Teachers in these schools are more likely than others to strongly agree that "teachers in a school share responsibility for the achievement of all students" and that "other teachers contribute to their success" in supporting their students' learning.

The survey also points to a higher level of trust in more collaborative schools (MetLife Inc., 2011, p. 17). Bryk and Schneider (2002) establish "relational trust" among teachers, as well as with administrators, parents, and students, as a "core resource" for school improvement. Without it, schools lack the "social capital" to change (Crowther, 2011; Hargreaves & Fullan, 2012).

Teachers also relate their collaboration with colleagues to improved student learning outcomes. The MetLife survey found that two thirds of the respondents believed that greater collaboration among teachers would have a "major impact" on improving student achievement. This perspective is borne out by a review of research on the impact of teachers' participation in professional learning communities (Vescio, Ross, & Adams, 2008); in all eight studies reviewed, researchers found that student learning improved:

> Although few in number, the collective results of these studies offer an unequivocal answer to the question about whether the literature supports the assumption that student learning increases when teachers participate in PLCs. The answer is a resounding and encouraging yes. (p. 87)

In a study of six high school critical friends groups (CFG) over three years, Curry (2008) asked whether possibilities for teacher learning such groups afforded outweighed the constraints. "From CFG insiders' [teachers'] perspectives," she concluded, "The answer to the question posed . . . would be, 'Yes!'" Roughly two thirds of her sample of twenty-five interviewees perceived CFGs in a "strongly positive" manner. She offered one teacher's response as emblematic: "From my viewpoint, it's the most significant professional development we have ever done in this building" (p. 768).

These finding are consistent with my own less formal survey of teachers over a dozen or so years about their participation in TLGs. Overwhelmingly, teachers have rated it as among the most, if not the most, powerful forms of professional development that they have experienced and the form most directly related to supporting students' learning. This is not to say that the practices of TLGs cannot become more effective in supporting teacher learning and instructional change—the subject of a discourse for researchers and practitioners to which this book seeks to contribute.

WHAT'S MISSING IN TLGS' PRACTICES?

Despite the positive reviews teachers regularly give their participation in TLGs, there have been important critiques of their effectiveness in supporting teacher learning, improving instructional practice, and contributing to greater student learning. As Little (2003) has observed, teachers' interactions in TLGs "both open up and close off opportunities for teacher learning and consideration of practice—in the same groups and sometimes at the same moments" (p. 935). In explaining how TLGs' work close off opportunities for learning, researchers have critiqued both the quality and content of the groups' discussions.

Curry (2008), in the study cited above, focused on how critical friends groups used discussion protocols to support their learning. The majority of teachers believed that the use of protocols significantly "enhanced the level of discourse and meaning constructed in CFG meetings" (p. 764). In Curry's view, however, the protocols tended to limit the groups' ability to investigate topics related to the participants' instructional practice and thus contributed to conversations that were often "shallow in their discussion of core instructional issues" (p. 768). She maintains the CFGs may suffer from trying to be "all things to all people" in terms of the kinds of professional development experiences teachers need, thus diluting the focus of the groups' collaborative efforts.

Bausmith and Barry (2011) point to a missing focus on "pedagogical content knowledge" (Shulman, 1987) in the discussions of many TLGs. They recommend that teachers' in-service professional development instead focus on videos of expert instruction aligned to curriculum standards. Such a recommendation signals a turnabout from the shift in professional development and goals for professional learning communities described above, relegating the responsibility for learning within the groups and schools to the realm of the "experts" from outside of it.

The question of what teachers learn through their participation in TLGs also has been addressed. In a study of teachers in the Netherlands, Meirink, Meijer, and Verloop (2007) sought to understand the changes in teachers' cognition or behavior as a result of their participation in TLGs. Their results suggest that the most commonly reported learning was equated with the confirmation of teachers' existing teaching method and that little of the learning was related to changes in behavior. This is consistent with the "proving stance" toward student-learning data assumed by teachers in many TLGs that Nelson, Slavit, and Deuel (2012) contrasted to the desired but rarer "inquiry stance" (more about this in the next section).

Constraints on TLGs' effectiveness come from outside the groups as well. Fullan (2008) perceived the work of many TLGs as "superficial." He attributed this to the relative absence of school administrators' capacity to support the groups' work. Too often, he maintains, establishing TLGs in a school offers a "false sense of progress, while deeper cultural changes required for school improvement are not tackled" (p. 28). As far back as 1990, Hargreaves and Dawe warned of the danger of "contrived collegiality," that is, teacher collaboration that seeks to satisfy administrative goals at the cost of the teachers' own autonomy and agency.

The likelihood of contrived collegiality has only increased given ever-mounting pressures on schools to demonstrate student achievement through improved standardized test scores, with a concomitant narrowing of the kinds of questions TLGs address and variety of practices they employ (Hargreaves & Fullan, 2012). In particular, greater emphasis is placed on the analysis of student achievement data, often from the standardized tests, in order to calibrate instruction that will improve achievement on the same measures, for example, to "adjust teaching, re-teach, and follow up on failing students" (Marshall, 2009, p. 171).

The nature of activity in groups will also be affected by a perception that their work is a hidden form of teacher evaluation rather than inquiry or, for that matter, collective creation. Such a perception makes it less likely teachers will expose problematic aspects of their instructional practice or their students' learning. One lesson from the theatre arts to be explored is how to welcome missteps as well as successes. If teachers do not feel safe to share their questions and unsuccessful strategies within their group, it is unlikely the group's activity will be substantive enough to affect participants' learning and individual teachers' classroom instruction.

THE PROBLEM OF TEACHER LEARNING

Why are some TLGs more effective than others in getting below the surface in their discussions of teaching and learning? One possible explanation, already alluded to, is that some groups approach their work with an "inquiry stance," that is, they manifest in their practices "a willingness to wonder, to ask questions, and to seek to understand by collaborating with others in the attempt to make answers to them" (Wells, 1999, p. 121). Teachers in groups with such a stance recognize that problems related to students' learning and their instruction are opportunities to deepen their knowledge and affect their practice rather than things to be avoided or solved as expeditiously as possible.

Can this stance really make a difference in teachers' learning and instructional improvement? In a study of participants in TLGs, Windschitl, Thompson, and Braaten (2011) found that the teachers who were more likely to develop new understandings and skills equated with "expert-like teaching" were those who they described as "teaching-learning problematic" (TL-P). These TL-P teachers conceived of their instructional dilemmas as "puzzles of practice," viewing teaching as inherently a matter of ambiguities and "improvisational instructional moves" (p. 7). In contrast, teachers who did not experience gains in expert-like teaching were characterized as "teaching-learning unproblematic" (TL-U), viewing teaching as a "problems with students" rather than problems to be investigated with colleagues.

The possibility for learning, thus, hinges on the way a teacher or a group views the myriad problems that come up in the practice of teaching. As Michael Fullan (1993) succinctly puts it: "Problems are our friends"; that is, if teachers are to create meaningful change in classrooms and schools, they must accept that uncertainty and even conflict are inevitable and even necessary.

Dewey (1916) described "the problem of teaching" as how to keep "the experience of the student moving in the direction of what the expert already knows" (p. 184). Perhaps the problem of teacher learning is how to keep the experience of the teachers moving in the direction of what they do not already know about teaching and learning. And doing so in a way that generates new directions and resources for both.

~

TLGs are the key vehicles for developing and deepening the schoolwide professional learning community, with its emphasis on reflective dialogue on practice, collaboration, and collective responsibility for students' learning. To do so, the groups employ structures and tools that guide and support their discussions, including inquiry cycles and protocols. There are many factors that affect the groups' effectiveness but perhaps primary among these is the group's own stance toward its activity.

The inquiry stance described in this chapter is a foundational mode of engagement for theatre artists, especially those that use methods for collective creation or devised theatre. The next chapter asks: what lessons for teacher learning do theatre artists offer in how they structure their work to enact that inquiry mode?

NOTE

1. The name Cooper Elementary School and the names of the teachers are pseudonyms.

2

The Theatrical Turn in Teacher Learning Groups

When I was about to step before my first high school English class, a seasoned teacher gave me this timeworn advice: "Act like you've been there before." It helped. Of course, the "acting" in that statement is not limited to what actors do on the stage; the same advice is regularly given to athletes. Still, it suggests a connection between what the teacher and actor do.

Teaching has long been compared to acting (Eisner, 1968; Labaree, 2010; Sarason, 1999). And while some comparisons have been fruitful, most have been limited by an exclusionary focus on the classroom as "stage" for the teacher as "educational performer" (John, 2006). For example, in *Acting Lessons for Teachers*, Tauber and Mester (2007) address the teacher's use of props, effective entrances to and exits from the classroom, and "blocking," that is, creating spatial relationships between the teacher and the students the way theatre companies do between actors.

These treatments largely ignore other dimensions of the actors' work, including the many ways in which they collaborate with each other, directors, designers, and writers in creating a piece for performance. Such comparisons, if carefully undertaken, might help us think critically about how teachers collaborate to develop their professional knowledge and improve instruction for their students.

This chapter addresses some of the ways theatre arts concepts and practices have been applied to teacher learning and instructional improvement, in particular: (1) rehearsal; (2) performance; and (3) the creation of experiences for students. It highlights studies that propose relationships between theatre arts ideas or practices and teacher learning. The chapter concludes by relating conceptualizations of teacher learning gleaned from the studies to influential theories of learning as socially situated, active, and constructivist—features that invite a deeper exploration of theatre arts practices.

REHEARSAL

Equating teaching with acting has given rise to a related theatre arts connection: teacher learning as rehearsal. Two studies offer different images of how the idea of rehearsal can be applied to the work of teachers—both preservice or in-service.

Coached Rehearsal

Sarah Scott (2008) focuses on a strategy called "coached rehearsal" in use during a literacy methods course that is part of an elementary teacher preparation program. She presents an extended transcript from one student teacher's coached rehearsal, during which she introduces the book she will read aloud to her students (played here by her peers). In the first part of the session, the teacher educator interrupts the student teacher frequently, proposing specific adjustments to her instructional approach, in many cases before she completes a sentence; for instance:

> Student teacher: So remember we left off on this page and we're going to start here and we're going . . .
> Teacher educator: So go back to the previous page. . . . (p. 8)

Directive comments like these from the teacher educator pepper the transcript. In the second part of a coached rehearsal, the teacher educator facilitates a full-group discussion about a problem that emerged in the earlier part for the student teacher being coached; in the example provided, the group discussed how to help actual students with technical language with which the teacher herself may not be familiar.

Scott concludes that coached rehearsals "disrupt what is typical in teacher education [by taking] a stance on expert practice, [interrupting] students while they were teaching, [and focusing] on the development of pedagogical skill in the university classroom rather than leaving it entirely 'for the field'" (p. 10). In this regard, coached rehearsal offers one model for the "approximations of practice," like those found in the training of ministers and clinical psychologists, that Grossman and colleagues (2009) found so lacking in teacher education (see introduction).

In its appropriation of the term rehearsal, however, the strategy does not reflect the complexity of rehearsal practices in the theatre arts—indeed, many contemporary directors would not recognize these session as rehearsal or, if so, as only one component of rehearsal. As the next chapter illustrates, rehearsal, while structured, is a much more open and exploratory experience for actors than it is for the student teachers in the episode from the literacy methods course. The director Anne Bogart (2001) writes:

> Rehearsal is not about forcing things to happen; rather it is about listening. The director listens to the actors. The actors listen to one another. You listen collectively to the text. You listen for clues. You keep things moving. You probe. . . . (p. 125)

In other words, rehearsal is understood as a form of collaborative inquiry and construction of knowledge, rather than the direct transmission of skills or knowledge.

Instructional Replays and Rehearsals

Ilana Horn (2010) offers a different application of rehearsal in her investigation of how high school math teachers learn from their interactions with peers in their school. She identifies two discourse structures that "position teachers to learn about teaching as they talk and work together" (p. 227): instructional replays and instructional rehearsals.

Instructional replays are retrospective accounts of specific classroom events, which often include "blow-by-blow renderings of interactions with students" (p. 239). In one example, Melinda, a student teacher, recounts to Guillermo, her mentor-teacher, an interaction with two students about how they respond to each other during group work. She tells her mentor-teacher she is concerned about whether students know how to respond when they ask each other questions in the groups:

> Cause like I was watching Angel ask David a question. And David kind of *tossed* an answer, he's like, "you do it this way." And it *clearly* didn't satisfy her, but she didn't come back with another question. And he didn't *register* that she hadn't processed, understood.

In addition to students' (and the teacher's) words, replays may also include their physical actions and emotions, as Horn's use of italics in the above quote is meant to signal.

Instructional rehearsals, by contrast, are forward-looking; they allow teachers to "project" both instructional moves they might make and their students' responses to them. These projections help teachers anticipate the kinds of interactions that may occur in their classrooms, in effect, serving as practice lessons, in which one teacher would "play the role of the teacher while others would play the role of the student" (p. 245). In response to Melinda's replay, above, and some elaboration of it prompted by his questions, Guillermo rehearses a possible teaching response: "Angel, it was great that you asked a question. David, you tried to answer it, but did you see what happened? Um, you gave an answer but you weren't checking to see whether you were really being helpful to Angel."

Rehearsals and replays like these are naturally occurring in conversation rather than events prompted by a facilitator or a protocol. Nevertheless, when they do occur, Horn contends they create spaces of "utilitarian make-believe" (Goffman, 1974). Such spaces allow for the "development of classroom interactional skills in a less consequential setting" (Horn, 2010, p. 245) than actual teaching—and a less pressured one than the coached rehearsals Scott describes. They offer a simulation, or projection, of practice rather than a strict approximation of it.

The value of such imaginative activities in the arts has long been recognized. For Maxine Greene (1986), these are "spaces in which particular atmospheres are created: atmospheres that foster active exploring rather than passivity, that allow for the unpredictable and the unforeseen." Greene goes on to point out that, "at once, there should be deliberately cultivated consciousness of craft, standard, and style" (p. 57), signaling that creativity does not emerge from random or undisciplined activity. While not consciously cultivated, the use of replays and rehearsals do model some of the qualities found in theatre artists' creative processes, including improvisation, role playing, and drawing on memories, observations, and images as materials with which to compose new work—all of which is explored in the next chapter.

PERFORMANCE

Several researchers have focused on the learning that occurs through actual performance. Their studies follow the pioneering work of the Brazilian theatre director and educator, Augusto Boal (1979, 1995), which engages participants in performances to confront and subvert social and psychological oppression.

Process Drama

A teacher educator with a background in acting, Tom Griggs (2001), examined the methods actors use to evoke character for an audience with an eye toward how preservice teachers might develop their own capacities to communicate with their students in ways that will positively affect their learning. He proposes using "process drama" methods with preservice teachers, including improvisational theatre games.

> Process drama provides a format for problem solving which requires group participation; it is a very purely collaborative form of drama, in which no predetermined outcome is to be reached, in which participants must balance originality/imagination/creativity with a concern for sustaining a "dramatic tension" with—and connection among—collaborators, in an effort to come to some sort of satisfactory resolution (i.e., "denouement") of the dramatic conflict introduced by the leader. (p. 33)

The use of such methods, he maintains, will allow preservice teaching candidates to address a wide range of issues and problems they might encounter in the classroom and, crucially, give the participants a chance to "stop, rewrite, rework, reconsider, and otherwise reflect upon more ideal resolutions to these dramatic conflicts than the undesirable ones which sometimes result" (p. 33). These actions—stop, rewrite, rework, and so forth—mirror those of theatre artists engaged in the process of collective collection, as chapter 3 reveals.

In another study that makes direct application of performance, Melisa Cahnmann-Taylor, Jennifer Wooten, Mariana Souto-Manning, and Jaime Dice (2009) describe the use "performance-based focus groups" with novice bilingual teachers to investigate and develop strategies to address professional conflicts they experience. The method draws explicitly on Boal's *Theatre of the Oppressed* (1979) and *Rainbow of Desire* (1985).

In one example, Marisol, a teacher of English for speakers of other languages (ESOL) performed a recurring problem that she had with another teacher who did not seem to care about the ESOL students in her class, which also includes mainstream students. In the scenario, Marisol acted out a situation in which she interrupted her colleague, who was shopping online, to ask about working with some of the ESOL students. Looking up from her monitor, the colleague tells Marisol, dismissively, "Keep the ESOL kids, keep them *all*!" (p. 2543). At this point, the arts-based researcher, serving as facilitator, asks Marisol to tell the group what she is feeling at that moment. Marisol expresses her frustration with her colleague: "I want to choke her. . . . Because it's not like she's, like, 'Oh, yeah someone is doing something good for them!' It's 'Thank God, I don't have to deal with them.'"

The researcher facilitator then invites others in the group to propose strategies to change the scenario for the better. As in Boal's methods, they do not simply offer it verbally; they must take Marisol's place in the scene and physically act it out. Jorge takes up the challenge and performs a different initial approach to the antagonist at her computer: "Hello, how are you?" Other strategies acted out by participants in the group include documenting the antagonist teacher's behavior and—one that did not meet the method's "reality check criteria for action"—destroying her computer (p. 2544).

Critical to the method employed here is the transcription by the researcher of the various possibilities enacted in the performances. The "tran/script" constitutes not just "artistic representations of data analysis or findings; rather, it becomes data to be analyzed by spect-acting participants in later focus groups." (p. 2555). In other words, the groups are creating materials that may be incorporated into later pieces.

The method mirrors practices common in collective creation or devised theatre of recording and transcribing improvisations or Composition pieces (Bogart & Landau, 2005) created by groups to use as materials in the development of the script for performance. It also demonstrates how teachers' collaboration can be deliberately structured to encourage the development of strategies and tools that teachers may apply in their own classrooms.

CREATION OF EXPERIENCES FOR STUDENTS

The last study discussed here does not explicitly refer to theatre practices or ideas at all, yet it takes us closer to how theatre artists create new pieces for performance. Rogers Hall (1996) describes the interaction of two student teachers developing a strategy to teach their students about adding rates of motion. He analyzes one fifty-seven-second episode (on videotape) from a significantly longer interaction. Using Dewey's notion of "*an* experience" as qualitatively different from the stream of experience that makes up everyday life, he relates the student teachers' creation of an experience for their students to the way an artist creates an experience for the viewer of his or her work so that it is "distinct and compelling for a designer (artist, teacher) and recipient (viewer, student) alike" (p. 213). For students to have compelling learning experiences, Hall argues, teachers must first undergo the experiences themselves.

One powerful way to undergo experiences is to create them. In trying to figure out how to teach the concept of adding rates of motion, the student teachers, identified as S and J, physically act out a collision. First, they take turns walking toward one another at slightly different rates; then S proposes they walk toward each other at the same rates, this time simultaneously (note: open brackets indicate onset of overlapping speech).

> S: (*S and J walk toward each other*) Then it'd be like we're goin' super, [we're goin' super, we're goin' like super, I'm going superfast.
>
> J: [(*they collide*, 1.5 sec elapsed) WOAH, We're goin' faster! RIGHT! (p. 220)

As Hall points out, the "surprise and engagement apparent in J's announcement of a qualitative difference" (p. 223) suggests that this is "an experience" for the pair—and one that offers possibilities for creating learning experiences for students.

Hall's account resonates strongly with the practices of theatre companies engaged in collective creation; there, actors are "writing on [their] feet" (Bogart & Landau, 2005), in other words, composing the script for performance rather than interpreting it. He also calls attention to the range and variety of resources, or materials, that are employed in the effort to produce an experience for others. In addition to what the student teachers say, these include the notes they write as they work and the movements, gestures, and physical interaction of S and J's activity. Along with text, image, and sound, these are some of the basic materials theatre artists use in their processes of collective creation.

LEARNING AS ACTIVITY, INQUIRY, AND CONSTRUCTION

While there are signal differences in how the studies described above employ theatre arts practices or ideas to teacher learning, together they project teacher learning as socially situated, inquiry-based, and constructivist. These same features underlie current conceptualizations of professional learning community and teacher inquiry.

The studies view teacher learning as socially situated *activity*, in which learning derives from interaction with others and participation in specific practices (Rogoff, Baker-Sennett, Lacasa, & Goldsmith, 1995; Vygotsky, 1978; Wenger, 1998; Wertsch, 1991). In this view, the interaction within teacher learning group (TLG) meetings functions as a primary site of professional learning. This does not exclude the classroom as a site of learning; indeed, the uses of theatre arts practices help us to see how classroom interactions are brought into TLG meetings as artifacts or evidence.

Teaching and learning interactions may also be the products of the group's activity: these may be simulated, as in the use of coached rehearsal, improvisations, and performance-based focus groups; recounted and projected, as in instructional replays; or imagined, as in instructional rehearsals and the student teachers' planning how to teach rates of motion.

Second, all view learning as *inquiry*, the active investigation of questions or problems related to instructional practice and student learning through experimentation, exploration of relationships, and reflection (Cochran-Smith & Lytle, 2009; Dewey, 1910). This view contrasts with one described in chapter 1 as "teaching-learning unproblematic," in which teaching is largely a matter of delivering a stable curriculum to groups of students. Instead, a "teaching-learning problematic" perspective treats classroom interactions as continual sources of problems for inquiry (Windschitl, Thompson, & Braaten, 2011).

Several of the studies engage theatre arts practices to enable the exploration and construction of possible responses to problems of practice, for example, the use of performance-based groups by the bilingual teachers and the pairing of replay of classroom interactions with rehearsal of possible teaching moves by the math teachers. Even coached rehearsal, which appears to be a very top-down, expert-to-novice form of instruction, culminates in a discussion of a problem identified during the simulation by the teacher who taught the lesson, which could provide an imaginative space for collective creation of possible instructional strategies.

Finally, and most significantly, the studies present teacher learning as *construction* of knowledge rather than *reproduction* of knowledge. As in communities of practice, learning reflects an ongoing rhythm of participation in social interaction and reification, that is, the creation of documents, systems, tools, and other artifacts that at once represent a "shared history of learning" and serve as resources for new learning (Lave & Wenger, 1991).

Here again, the application of theatre arts practices, which continually enable the creation of performances-as-products, helps us to appreciate the products of TLGs' activity. These may include learning experiences for students, akin to the experience of the student teachers working on rates of motion; new possibilities for dealing with an obstreperous peer, like the ones the bilingual teachers performed; or the identification of problems for continued inquiry, like that of introducing students to technical language that emerged in the coached rehearsal session. In all these examples, teachers are creating their own learning as products to be performed with and for their colleagues and their students.

~

The studies described in this chapter each relate teacher learning to theatre arts ideas or practices, focusing on rehearsal, performance, and creating experiences for others. Collectively, they depict teacher learning as a social activity that is constructivist and fundamentally inquiry oriented.

These same features describe the work of theatre artists engaged in collective creation. The next chapter builds on these efforts to relate teacher learning to theatre arts ideas and practices through a sustained exploration of collective creation in the theatre arts.

3

Collective Creation in the Black Box

In a 2008 interview on National Public Radio, Todd Kreidler described working with his friend and collaborator, the playwright August Wilson, who had recently passed away:

> A typical day? My cell phone rings at eight o'clock in the morning: "Hey man, what you doing man? You up?" "Yeah." "You want to get some breakfast?" "Sure." "I'll meet you at the spot." Now, see, the spot was, whatever city we were in, where we would hang out and start our day for breakfast. So it was Cartons in Chicago, The Mecca in Seattle, here in D.C. it was Cupa Cupa. I mean every city had a spot and that's where we'd start our day. And every day we'd start off with at least three elements. We always had music. We always had the newspaper. And we always had stories. The newspaper would always launch something.

This anecdote reconnects us to the framework for collective creation described in the introduction. In it are glimpses of all three elements: *Means* describes the structures and tools theatre artists employ for their collaborative activity; for Wilson and Kreidler, this includes the rituals of their breakfast meetings and the music that provided a soundtrack for the conversation. The element of *materials* describes the variety of sources they draw upon: stories, items from that day's newspaper, and music (again). *Modes of engagement* describes the orientation or stance toward one another and toward their collective activity.

Clearly, the mode of their conversations is that of friendly, even playful, exchange; however, that mode is inflected with the expectation that riffing on newspaper stories would "launch" something, in other words, generate new ideas to be pursued through more formal theatre arts practices.

Theatre artists will deliberately and intensively apply these same three elements in the studio or black box spaces as they create new pieces for performance, including plays, dances, and other pieces. This chapter elaborates the means-materials-modes of engagement framework through the work of contemporary theatre artists. For each of the elements, it provides examples of specific practices that contribute to the composition of a new piece for performance. And while it does not discuss the practices in these terms, it is clear that they model the socially situated, inquiry-based, and constructivist features of communities of practice and other forms of learning through participation described in the previous chapter.

The focus here is on theatre artists and theatre arts companies that practice collective creation (Chen, Pulinkala, & Robinson, 2010) or devised theatre (Oddey, 1994). With these methods, there is often no existing script for the director or actors to interpret. Instead, the piece for performance is collaboratively developed through ongoing interaction among participants in a group, which typically includes a director, designers, and actors. In some cases, groups work with a writer as well.

Anne Bogart's practices are particularly important to the development of the framework for collective creation. They are widely used in theatre arts and well documented (Bogart & Landau, 2005; Cummings, 2006). I also draw on my own experiences as a participant in workshops conducted by the Ghost Road Company of Los Angeles and the Pig Iron Theatre Company of Philadelphia, whose methods are consistent with Bogart's. The chapter concludes with a vignette from the Ghost Road Company workshop that demonstrates how the elements of the framework overlap and interact.

MEANS

While chance, like luck, undoubtedly plays a part in the creation of new work, theatre artists leave little to chance. Instead, they employ explicit processes for collective creation. These processes specify the "components for rigorous creation" (Rabinow, 2011, p. 131) that enable the artists' work to be generative, that is, to lead to the creation of a complete piece for performance.

The framework element of means designates three such components: (1) structures to initiate and guide the process of creating new work; (2) tools that promote generative collaboration at specific points in the process; and (3) roles that affect how the structure and tools are employed.

Structures

Anne Bogart and Tina Landau's (2005) Composition method provides one influential and widely used structure for creating new work; its steps are (1) Identify the basic building blocks for devised work; (2) Gathering material related to the building blocks; (3) Lateral thinking; (4) Composition; (5) Assign and create; and (6) Present and discuss.

The process begins with *identifying the basic building blocks* for the creation of the work, in particular, articulating a question that the group (actors, director, designers) will collectively explore. While the question may change over time, it remains a guiding vector for the group's creation process. For example, the question that initiated the development of the SITI Company's *Culture of Desire* (1997–1998) was, "Who are we becoming in light of the pervasive and rampant consumerism that permeates our every move through life?" (Bogart & Landau, 2005, p. 154).

In the Ghost Road Company workshop described later in the chapter, the question was: "What do we choose to pay attention to [in this world]—and choose to ignore?" From these examples, it should be clear that the question must be provocative to the participants and sufficiently open-ended to sustain inquiry over time.

The next step in the process is *to gather materials,* which involves identifying sources of all kinds that relate to the question. "Source work" may be conducted collectively or individually and might involve interviews and other traditional research methods, seeking out images and objects, generating new texts, and many more. It is easy to imagine how the questions above would prompt participants to scour the Internet and other sources (film, television, magazines, etc.) for images and texts that reflect consumerism and celebrity worship in our society.

In the Ghost Road Company's methods, the company member who instigates the project, whether an actor or Katharine Noon, the company's director, brings an initial set of materials for the rest of the company to respond to:

> This research is riffing off the source material and the initial research of the instigating artist. The company will have inspirations about the work sparked by their own life experience. This research, which can range from articles, to images, to fiction, to music, can sometimes be tangential to the original questions proposed, but it is an important step in thinking broadly about what has been presented before the process of narrowing the scope of the development begins. (Noon, 2011)

Figure 3.1 shows actors from the Ghost Road Company and Studium Teatralne of Poland sharing images early in a collaborative composition process.

The possibilities identified through "riffing off of source materials" relates to the step Bogart and Landau (2005), borrowing from Edward de Bono (1990), call "*lateral thinking*." This step involves "freely associating off one another's ideas" (p. 156); its purpose is to generate "new and exciting ideas about what might happen within that arena" (p. 156), that is, the piece they are collaboratively generating. Some of these ideas will be picked up on in later stages of the process, others let go.

A "generating tool" used by the Pig Iron Theatre Company is "Open Canvas," in which a specified number of participants face each other across the studio floor. The director of the exercise gives the performers a question or phrase to respond to, for example, "missed connections." The actors begin to improvise, sometimes individually but ultimately in relation to one another.

The director may call out, "All off but X" or "X and Y" if she sees promising action or interaction develop, and gradually the other actors will respond to this. Quinn Bauriedel (2012), co-artistic director of the company, describes the method as "an early exercise that we do a lot in the first portion of the process to put all of the thinking and all the ideas into action on stage. . . . We have the real belief that we certainly could sit around all day talking to each other about the ideas, but it doesn't really matter until they see the light of day on the stage, so we try to talk less and do more."

Steps 4 and 5 of Bogart and Landau's process, *composition* and *assign and create,* are tightly coupled. In Composition, the director or someone else in the company gives the group an "assignment" or "[puzzle] that the group might solve" (p. 157). All groups are assigned the same "ingredients" that

FIGURE 3.1
Sharing images. The Ghost Road Company, Los Angeles.

must be included, in some way, in their piece. The ingredients, which often reflect possibilities identified earlier through source work and lateral thinking, might include specific fragments of text, gestures, props, songs, and so on. The product of each group's work is a unique composition addressing the common assignment and incorporating the specified ingredients.

These assignments are intended to develop the "theatre vocabulary that will be used for any given piece" (Bogart & Landau, 2005, pp. 12–13), that is, the dialogue, movement, and images that together constitute the finished play. Making compositions forces artists to "[write] on your feet" (Bogart & Landau, 2005), leaving the table and physically trying out possibilities. This approach was illustrated in the last chapter by the student teachers planning how to teach rates of motion and the bilingual teachers acting out alternative approaches to a disrespectful colleague.

The final step of the process is to *present and discuss* the compositions after they are performed. The director invites observers (usually those who have or will perform their own pieces) to "recognize any risks that were incurred [and] list the pitfalls that came up and welcome discoveries of what to avoid while putting together the production at hand" (Bogart & Landau, 2005, p. 160). The goal of these reflective activities is to identify elements ("vocabulary") that can be used in going forward with the development of the final piece.

Tools

In a discussion with Anne Bogart, the playwright Charles Mee (Mee & Bogart, 2007) described an early stage in the development of the play *Hotel Cassiopeia*, based on the life and work of artist Joseph Cornell, he developed in collaboration with the SITI Company:

> I walk into a room with [actors and designers]: "Here's a list of 15 images I get from Cornell. . . . Now you guys go make lists. We take two from column A, one from column B. . . . They make their compositions. Then I take all that stuff home with me.

Without using the word, Mee is describing specific tools he and his collaborators use within a larger structure of collective creation. So, for example, for the step of source work, a tool might be creating lists; for lateral thinking, sharing the lists and selecting items from different lists; and for composition, using the selections as ingredients in creating and reflecting on compositions (using Bogart and Landau's methods described above).

Tools may be elaborate, like the Composition assignments with their many required ingredients. Or they may be as simple as a way of discussing something. In working with a group of university theatre students on performing

Shakespeare, the Irish actress Fiona Shaw asks the students to comment on a colleague's performance of a soliloquy: "What does it do that it's so good?" Bauriedel asks observers of an Open Canvas improvisation (Open University, 1999), "What *arrests* you?" Both questions serve as tools to isolate effective elements of performance, ones that might be incorporated in a larger piece.

Another Means

Before examining roles, the third component of means, let us consider another influential structure for collective creation. Developed by landscape architect Lawrence Halprin and used by his wife, choreographer Anna Halprin, and then other theatre artists, the RSVP Cycles are intended to facilitate communication among participants during collaborative processes of all kinds. (See figure 3.2.) Its components are resources, scores, valuaction, and performances.

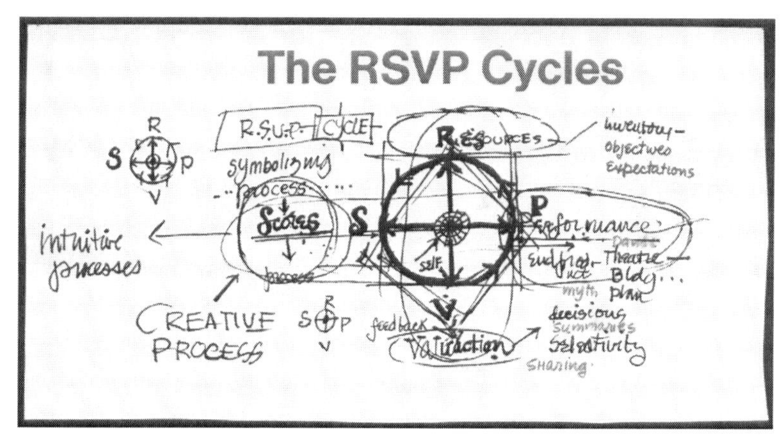

FIGURE 3.2
The RSVP Cycles. Lawrence Halprin Collection, the Architectural Archives, University of Pennsylvania. Used with permission.

Resources is an intentionally broadly inclusive category. For Anna Halprin, the resources for collective creation are both "physical" and "human," and include "movements, motivation, space, number of people, etc." (Worth & Poyner, 2004, p. 122). While Bogart and Landau distinguish the questions or themes that initiate and motivate a process of creation from the materials that address these "building blocks," the RSVP Cycles treat these as one type of resource among the many other types that participants may draw upon in their collaboration.

Scores are frameworks for activity that make it possible for a group to carry out its intended activity, as a musical score does for a group of musicians. The score may be visual (as in a map or a chart), verbal (as in a list or an outline), or indeed musical. Whatever form it takes, a score will be "open" or "closed":

> Open scores tend to be frameworks for action—reference points that allow the person for whom the score is written to include his own input, his own ideas, his own objectives. Closed scores are goal-oriented and dictatorial while open scores are objective-oriented and democratic. (Halprin & Burns, 1974, p. 33)

In other words, an open score initiates and guides activity without imposing predetermined outcomes or products.

Valuaction denotes "the value of the action." It describes how the ongoing process for collective creation incorporates "appreciation, feedback, value building and decision-making" (Halprin, 1995, p. 23). In the creation of a dance, participants in Halprin's company might comment on "specific elements of the dance that helped or hindered them as well as the overall demands of working in this overall format" (Worth & Poyner, 2004, p. 121). The point of valuaction is not to provide an overall evaluation of the piece, but rather to identify specific elements that will contribute to the finished piece, much as Shaw or Bauriedel's questions do.

Performance refers to how the score is actually enacted and how the resources are employed. And while the "P" comes at the end of the acronym "RSVP," it refers to performances at any point in the creation process, for example, the Composition pieces Bogart's actors make or the improvisations created in the Open Canvas activity used by the Pig Iron Company. Performance, thus, provides the basis for valuaction, which identifies specific ways the piece and the process might be developed, including providing ideas for different resources (materials) and scores to enable new performances—thus the RSVP *Cycles*.

As in Bogart and Landau's steps for Composition, the components of the RSVP Cycles here can be appreciated as a set of tools to support activity at specific points within an overall structure for collective creation. This is perhaps particularly clear with how scores foster communication among participants. Some scores, like some Composition exercises, are elaborate; for example, the score for "Vortex," a part of Halprin's larger *Circle of the Earth* dance, specified these activities:

- Walk.
- Cooperate in finding a collective pulse.
- Develop a personal walking movement to the collective pulse.
- Evolve your dance.
- Move in lines, circles, levels, areas, between, over, under, around.
- Join and rejoin with other people, and other groups.
- Build a mountain of people and other groups. (Worth & Poyner, 2004, pp. 117–18)

Effective scores also can be quite simple and respond to the activity of the group as it unfolds. In creating *Dancing with Life on the Line*, Halprin worked with nondancers who were HIV positive. When she found participants were experiencing challenges in working together, she decided to introduce a new score within the work that called for each of the individual participants in the group to call out to another participant in the group to support them and to tell them why they have chosen them to do so. This simple score "facilitated the speaking of many powerful and hidden truths" (Worth & Poyner, 2004, p. 133); it both enabled communication and contributed to the collective development of the piece.

The capacity to create a score in response to activity within the group is an important function of roles, the final dimension of means—as critical for the facilitator of a teacher learning group (TLG) as it is for the director of a theatre arts company engaged in collective creation.

Roles

As a component of means, roles does not refer to the parts actors portray in a given piece, but rather to the functions individuals enact within the group that contribute to collective creation of a piece for performance. It goes without saying that the director plays the most powerful and significant role in creating a piece for performance. But theatre artists, including Augusto Boal (1979) and Dario Fo (1987), have long challenged the traditional role of director as the genius who conveys, often in the most authoritarian fashion, his or her vision of the play script to the audience via actors, sets, costumes, and music (Knowles, 2004). Instead, they emphasize the creative role of the performers—and even blur the distinction between spectator and performer.

Bogart (2001), too, has reflected on the nature of the director's role in creating new work, arguing that the role not be equated with the individual but rather distributed among participants in the company or group: "Being a director is a function rather than a person. It is a way of seeing, analyzing, creating meaning, and contributing to the situation" (p. 34). Thus, as in the vignette from Bogart's Collaboration class in the introduction, the director asks questions and offers resources to the actors but also makes space for others to do the same.

The director, though, has the unique responsibility within the company to care for the process of collective creation itself, in other words, "create the circumstances in which something might happen" (Bogart, 2001, p. 124). Creating circumstances includes determining which tool to use at a particular stage of the creation process, for example, generating lists, doing an Open Canvas activity, or creating compositions. All of these and many other tools, or "scores," create a space within which collaborative activity can occur.

Bogart points to another dimension of the director's role—one that may seem contradictory to ideas of collaboration as sharing perspectives and building on one other's ideas—that is, to "awaken opposition and disagreement," even as you "take care of the quality of space and time between yourself and others" (p. 105). Bogart and other theatre artists recognize that collaboration generative of new work will involve and value disagreement, challenging one another's ideas, seeking out and exploiting fissures in the group's understanding. Without these gaps, there is no possibility for creating something new: "When things start to fall apart in rehearsal, the possibility of creation exists" (p. 86).

To encourage possibilities for creation, the director may highlight or even create obstacles. This is one reason for the long list of "ingredients" she gives groups to include in creating their compositions and for the very brief amount of time they have to do so. This creates an "Exquisite Pressure [which] comes from an environment where forces lean on the participants in a way that enables more, not less, creativity" (Bogart & Landau, 2005, p. 138). Managed well, the constraints of exquisite pressure become allies in collective creation, a topic for chapter 5.

In observing Bogart, Noon, and other directors at work, it is evident that they seek to create a space for offering and challenging ideas—but a space within which it is always safe to do so. Bogart ritually ends the feedback after a series of compositions by asking: "Everybody OK?"

I experienced a similar concern for my group's and my own physical and emotional well-being throughout the Ghost Road Company workshop (described later in the chapter). The leaders continually adjusted their process in response to the group's strengths and needs, for example, introducing Composition exercises earlier than they expected, while, at the same time, limiting the list of "ingredients" each group would be required to include within their piece (Noon, 2011).

In the Pig Iron Theatre Company workshop, which involved much more intensive physical movement, the participants were continually stretched in what they could accomplish. But they were always supported by one another and the workshop leader, that is, the exercises built in physical and emotional support.

MATERIALS

In an episode of the Canadian television program, *Slings and Arrows*, set at a fictionalized Stratford Theatre Festival, a young movie star makes his first-ever stage appearance, as Hamlet, no less. After a tumultuous rehearsal process, he is about to make first entrance on opening night. He turns to his director and says, "I feel sick to my stomach." Without missing a beat, the director instructs him: "Use it!"

"Use everything" is a familiar theatre arts maxim. Indeed, both Bogart and Landau's methods and the RSVP Cycles highlight the extraordinary importance of the "stuff" artists employ in creating new work. With Bogart and Landau's methods, source work describes the stage of gathering materials related to the initiating question; the RSVP Cycles begin with attention to resources of all kinds, human and physical. Without a rich set of materials to mine, these methods proclaim, no amount of technique, talent, and time will result in creation of a new work.

In *Art as Experience*, Dewey (1934) differentiated between "inner" materials and "outer" materials, claiming both as essential to the creation of art. *Outer materials* constitute those physical artifacts one can pick up, point to, listen to, and so on. A paradigmatic example of outer materials might be poor Yorick's skull, which Hamlet holds in his hand and addresses.

Inner materials, by contrast, are ideational or representational; for Dewey, the category is exemplified by "images, observations, memories, and emotions" (p. 77). The butterflies in the stomach of the young actor count as materials, as do the emotions expressed by the nonactors in the score devised by Anna Halprin, described above.

Bogart and Landau (2005) provide an example of how source work can compel the identification of inner materials for a company to use.

> When Tina visited Anne in rehearsal for Strindberg (a piece she made about August Strindberg's world . . .), Anne was in the middle of Source Work with the company. She had asked the actors to fill in the blanks: "When I think of Strindberg, I see _____, I hear _____, I smell _____, etc." On the day Tina visited they were reading their lists out loud. The were full of images of men in top hats and women in long gowns of crimson and black velvet, Edvard Munch paintings, the sound of a piano playing, a clock ticking. (p. 166)

A similar approach was evident in the lists Charles Mee asked collaborators to write out in their response to Joseph Cornell's work.

The Ghost Road Company uses brief "free writing" exercises as a tool for generating materials (as we will see later in the chapter). For five or so minutes, company members individually respond in writing to a question or other prompt, then read their pieces aloud to the group. Since free writes often elicit memories, emotions, or images, they are particularly effective in identifying those inner images that might be overlooked in the creation process.

Of course, existing texts also provide materials for collective creation: these might be excerpts from newspaper stories, poems, stories, songs, blogs, television commercials, and on and on. In fact, devised theatre pieces are sometimes described as collages, given the intentional variety of materials on which they draw.

In these examples, structure, tools, and materials coalesce in collective creation: once the company has a question or theme to initiate its work, it moves to source work, that is, the identification and generation of materials related to the question or theme. Source work can only be realized through the use of specific tools, such as Bogart's fill-in-the-blanks activity, Mee's lists, or the Ghost Road Company free writing prompts.

What is identified or generated using these tools become the materials for the next steps in the structure: exploring relationships through lateral thinking, composing pieces, and performing and discussing these.

MODES OF ENGAGEMENT

In an essay on Michel Foucault, the anthropologist Paul Rabinow (2011) writes:

> The metric of thought did not consist uniquely in an act of diagnosis (or representation) for its own sake but rather included the effort to achieve a modal change from seeing a situation not only as "a given" but equally as "a question." Thinking is an act of modal transformation from the constative to the subjunctive: from the singular to the multiple, from the necessary to the contingent. (pp. 88–89)

Such a "modal change" in thinking, from constative—declaring that this is the case—to subjunctive—embracing contingency and possibility—resonates with Maxine Greene's (1986) description of imaginative spaces "in which particular atmospheres are created: atmospheres that foster active exploring rather than passivity, that allow for the unpredictable and the unforeseen" (p. 57).

Activity, whether individual or collective, is unshackled from the realization of a predetermined outcome. Instead, it embraces questions and problems, exploration of multiple possibilities—some of which may prove fruitful, some not—and a welcoming of unforeseen contingencies and opportunities, the very dispositions of those teachers, identified in chapter 1, who view teaching and learning as "problematic" (and that that's a good thing!).

Modes of engagement, as an element of the framework, highlight the orientation a group takes to its own activity, for example, the playful but productive exchange of Wilson and Kreidler's breakfast meetings. For theatre artists whose methods are fundamentally collaborative, three modes essential to collective creation are critically important: (1) inquiry; (2) serious play; and (3) "Yes, and. . . ."

INQUIRY

In collective creation, there is often no existing play script to use as a starting point. Instead, the process begins with questions that provoke the company to explore multiple and alternate possibilities, to experiment, and even to welcome missteps as a necessary part of the creation process. These activities are at the heart of what we mean by inquiry, whether we are talking about theatre artists, scientists, or TLGs like those described in this book.

To have meaningful inquiry, theatre artists recognize, there must be interest. In speaking about the initiating question(s) for a production, Katharine

Noon (2001) says, "This is the part of the process where I say to company members, 'This is what I'm interested in. Are you interested?'" Bogart (2001), too, links an artist's interest to the questions that initiate and guide a creative process, a process she describes explicitly as inquiry:

> Interest is the artist's primary tool and it occupies the territory of personal insecurity—you do not have the answers and are provoked by the questions. . . . In the exquisite moments of curiosity and interest, we live between, we travel outward with inquiry. Interest is a feeling directed outward toward an object or a person or a subject, a theme, or a play. (p. 131)

Curiosity and interest are sparked by questions, which in turn can be channeled into creation through various forms of work—and play.

SERIOUS PLAY

"There is a place for discussion, for research, for the study of history and documents, as there is a place for roaring and howling and rolling on the floor," (p. 125) the influential director Peter Brook (1968) writes of developing a play. Methods for collective creation, such as Bogart and Landau's and the RSVP Cycles, continually make space for playing. For instance, a common direction from Anne Bogart to actors working on a scene is "do something dumb." Her actors understand this not as an invitation to make a mistake, but as a strategy for suddenly changing things up, interjecting something new—whether a line of dialogue, a gesture, a prop, or so on—playing with the piece to force the players to respond in new and potentially fruitful ways.

Theatre games, like those gently satirized in Annie Baker's 2009 play *Circle Mirror Transformation*, are essential tools used by theatre artists to generate materials for the pieces they are developing. In working with student actors, Fiona Shaw has each choose an animal for which to improvise movement. After a good deal of crawling around, clucking, and growling, she asks one who has chosen to be a crocodile to speak one of Macbeth's soliloquies *as his animal* (Open University, 1999). The playfulness of the approach results in some surprising, and quite serious, possibilities for how the speech might be delivered in a production.

"YES, AND . . ."

How do theatre artists achieve the rigor and discipline to make play coherent and generative? One of the most time-honored principles for improvisation is "Yes, and . . . ," which compels the actors working with a group to accept (i.e., literally and figuratively to say "yes") and elaborate on ("and . . .") their collaborators' "complementary offers," or "turns." A turn might take the form of a question, statement, movement, or gesture (e.g., a shrug). There are many ways an actor might accept and elaborate, for example, by parrying it, transforming it, quoting it, parodying it, demonstrating its inverse, and so on.

Actors speak of how specific turns contribute to "extending . . . heightening, and raising the stakes" (Sawyer, 2003, pp. 94–95), signifying how they simultaneously move the action forward while promoting inclusion and responsiveness to one another. When an actor rejects a collaborator's turn to introduce something new and unrelated, the development of the piece sputters.

The mode of "Yes, and . . ." is evident in specific generating exercises, such as Open Canvas, but it is present throughout the creation of a piece. It encourages all participants to see themselves as contributors to the development of the piece rather than merely interpreters of someone else's text or vision. It also signals an important dynamic between the individual and the group, which Bogart (2001) describes here:

> To create we must set ourselves apart from each other. This does not mean that "No, I don't like your approach, or your ideas." It does not mean that "No, I won't do what you are asking me to do." It means "Yes, I will include your suggestion, but I will come at it from another angle and add these new notions." (p. 89)

Merely going along with the group is not sufficient. A young director participating in a SITI Company intensive training recalled how Bogart had pointed out to him that there is "disagreement that stops the process and disagreement that moves the process forward, healthy disagreement" (Evans, 2006).

One of the director's responsibilities is to highlight disagreements as they emerge in such a way that they may become generative. As we'll see in the chapters that follow, the same responsibilities will be critical to collective creation processes of TLGs.

While these modes can be treated separately, they only contribute to collective creation if they coexist and reinforce one another. Practicing "Yes, and . . ." within an improvisation or in creating a composition should exemplify the mode of serious play—indeed, it may often include some "rolling on the floor and howling." And play itself is profoundly related to inquiry; as

Manfred Wekwerth (2011), a collaborator of Bertolt Brecht, writes: "'Wondering' is the source of all discovery, all inspirations, all humour, in Brecht's theatre (and not only there). And thus of all enjoyment" (p. 45). That spirit of enjoyment, which eventually is shared with an audience, begins with the pleasure the company members take in the creating of the piece—in a coffee shop with music and newspapers or in the rehearsal studio.

The next section offers a vignette from a workshop in which I participated to demonstrate how means, materials, and modes of engagement interact within the collective creation process.

MAKING A COMPOSITION

The Ko Theatre Festival at Amherst College is an annual summer celebration of theatre with performances from companies from the United States and abroad. It is also a school for collective creation, as several of the performing theatre artists or companies give workshops on their methods. The workshop described here was conducted by Katharine Noon, artistic director of the Ghost Road Company of Los Angeles, and two company members, Brian Weir and Christel Joy Johnson. There were sixteen participants, including me, with widely varied levels of experience with performance and directing.

On the first day, Katharine told the group that the company's process for creating a piece begins with a question to explore, along with "extant texts" related to the question, identified by a company member who has done some initial research on the question. She introduced the question for our work: "What do we choose to pay attention to—and choose to ignore?" She also provided us with three texts: a reproduction of Breughel's painting *Landscape with the Fall of Icarus* and two poems that respond to the painting—one by W. H. Auden and the other by William Carlos Williams.

The first day was mostly spent in doing a series of "free writes" related to the question and the extant texts. For each, Katharine gave us a brief prompt, then we would write for about five minutes. Then, in turn and without commentary, we would read our free writes to the group. The Ghost Road Company members took notes and later collected our free write texts; excerpts from some of these texts would provide materials for later steps in the process.

In preparation for the next day's session, Katharine asked us to identify and bring in photographs, images, or objects related to the initiating question or to the texts. We used these images as materials for another round of free writes and read alouds. In the afternoon, we worked on "snapshots," or wordless tableaux. In groups of three, we selected an excerpt from one of our free write texts to present in three parts (with five- to ten-second "blackouts" called by Katharine between sections during which observers simply closed their eyes).

Later, we each selected one object from all those gathered and used it in multiple ways to tell the story of Icarus. I used sheets of newspaper to create an island, a wing, and a shroud. After each round of snapshots, we sat in a circle and talked about specific moments or images that stood out for us. Katharine explained that some of these, along with excerpts from the free writes, would be incorporated in the lists of "ingredients" for the next day's Composition exercises.

On the third day, we were assigned groups of about five and given just ninety minutes to complete a composition, which we would then perform for the rest of the group. Each of the groups' Composition pieces had to include the following "ingredients":

- Four separate sections: (1) What do we choose to pay attention to in this world? (2) What are the consequences of that? (3) What do we choose to ignore in this world? (4) What are the consequences of that?
- Elements: use of technology; recorded music; rhythmic sound; "near and far"; "high and low"; an act of defiance; an act of cruelty; one gesture repeated ten times; ten seconds of stillness; a discovery; an accident; air and water in excess; use of one image [from those we had gathered].
- Four lines of text: (1) "I knew how to fly even though I'd never flown" (from a free write); (2) "Flying low—skinny boy—three feet above the ground" (free write); (3) "It's always easier to be the armchair traveler" (free write); (4) "How everything turns away quite leisurely from the disaster" (from Auden poem).

Neither Katharine nor her company members elaborated on the ingredients or explained how we were to use them. "Every composition is a big fat experiment," she told us, and exhorted us to "get on your feet as soon as you can—don't spend too much time talking."

My group consisted of Dorothy, Carla, Alexandra (Alex), and Beth. Some had extensive experience with performance, others, like me, very little. We decided to begin by each selecting one image from those gathered during the second day's source work. This might at least help us to satisfy one of the required elements.

As we sat back down with our images, Dorothy offered an idea for part of our composition. She had selected a photograph of outstretched hands. Her idea, she told us, was to do something with baseball, specifically a boy sliding into a base. This would allow us to incorporate one of the required lines of text: "Flying low—skinny boy—three feet above the ground" and the element "high and low." To me, this felt like a premature shaping of the piece, but I remembered Katharine's last guideline: "Don't say no to an idea until you talk it through. Say 'Yes, and . . . '" We agreed that the idea of baseball and games would be one to explore.

Since it was a beautiful day, we decided to create and perform our piece on the grassy quadrangle outside the building we'd been working in. We grabbed objects from the studio, not sure how or if we would use them, including pieces of fabric, a tennis ball, pieces of white and colored paper, a water bottle, and others. As we talked about how we might do something with the baseball game idea, I picked up the tennis ball, tossed it underhand into the air, and caught it, saying, "This might be a way to bring in the repeated gesture"—one of the required ingredients.

Somebody else suggested a game of catch between two players, and Alex and I started to act it out. We liked this (moving) image, but what did it have to do with our question for the first section: "What do we choose to pay attention to in this world?"

We started to build a scenario around the game of catch: As Alex and I tossed the ball to each other, fooling around with different speeds and trajectories, the others became fans at a game. As we passed the ball back and forth, the spectators' eyes followed it like a metronome hand. I tried out the idea of pocketing the ball and mimed throwing it, and Alex followed suit. The fans continued to track its imagined arc. As they did so, Carla called out one of the lines of required text: "It's always easier to be the armchair traveler."

We created a dialogue among the hyperattentive spectators, alternating the "armchair traveler" line with the "skinny boy" one to demonstrate what "we" (the fans) choose to pay attention to and what the consequences are, in this case, missing the disappearance of the ball itself. We had our first section!

Work on the next section was sparked by the idea of using a paper airplane to include the required elements of "high and low" and "near and far." After a few laughable attempts to get our planes to fly outdoors, Carla and Beth improvised a kind of puppet show effect: they held up a blue cloth representing the sky, and Carla manipulated a paper airplane in loops in front of it, eventually simulating a slow-motion crash. (See figure 3.3.)

We decided the plane crash would go unnoticed by the spectators, whose attention was still centered on Alex as the star player. The fans would crowd around her after our mimed game of catch had finished, while I scowled enviously from afar. "I knew how to fly even though I'd never flown," she threw off in a self-important and dismissive tone of voice. We incorporated the "act of cruelty" by having Alex, growing bored with signing autographs, turn away from her fans and, spitefully, stomping on the crash-landed paper plane. Second section composed.

An onslaught of bees, an allergic participant, and a move inside curtailed our work on a third section, so we performed the two that we had completed.

FIGURE 3.3
Making a composition. Photo by Christel Joy Johnson.

Means, Materials, and Modes at Work and Play

The episode of (interrupted) composition allows us to see each of the elements of the framework for collective creation in action, as well as how they cohere in the creative process. All three components of *means* are evident: structure, tools, and roles. The structure for the full group's process began with the sharing of the question and extant texts (painting and poems), and proceeded to the free writes, snapshots, and compositions. The structure of the process extended beyond what is described in the vignette to the creation of a play script, by Katharine, Brian, and Christel, rehearsals, and a single performance for an ad hoc audience on the last of the workshop.

Specific tools used at different stages within the structure included the initiating question, free writes and read alouds, snapshots, and the Composition assignment. Each of these tools generated materials (text, images, movements, etc.) that were used in the next step of the process. So, for example, the lines about "the armchair traveler" and "skinny boy—flying low" came from the first-day free write exercises and became required ingredients (materials) for the group Composition exercises described above. Images from these, such as use of sheets for shrouding (from a second round of compositions making), in turn were incorporated in our final whole-group piece for performance.

Katharine, as director, played a clear role in framing the question (and selecting initial texts) to initiate the creation process. Along with Brian and Christel, she also selected specific elements from the free writes, snapshots, and extant texts (especially lines from the poems) to become "ingredients" in the compositions. She took the lead, working with Christel and Brian, in creating the play script, assigning parts, and leading rehearsals. Throughout the rehearsals, she invited input from all the participants.

The episode reveals an array of *materials*. Outer materials included the painting and poems selected by Katharine, and the photographs and objects identified by participants (for example, the photo of hands, the tennis ball, and blue fabric that became the sky for our paper plane). Inner materials, including memories or emotions, were elicited through the free write exercises, for example, the line "I knew how to fly even though I'd never flown." They were also given shape through the snapshots and compositions created by individuals and groups, for example, the attitudes of the spectators to the baseball star and the plane crash.

The creation of the composition also reflects the three *modes of engagement* identified above: inquiry, serious play, and "Yes, and. . . ." We seem to have been more provoked by interest, for example, in an image of a baseball game, than attention to the initiating question for the workshop, "What do we choose to pay attention to [in this world]?" or to the questions Katharine had given us to focus individual sections on. However, as we started to work on our feet, our mode became increasingly inflected by inquiry as we discussed what spectators at the baseball game pay attention to and ignore, which ultimately affected how we staged that section and the subsequent section of the piece.

The mode of serious play was evident throughout. If my own experience is a measure, I can report a productive tension of stress (How are we going to get this done in so little time?) and physical and mental pleasure in the process of trying out ideas through movement and speech. Examples of serious play can be seen in both our comical, but ultimately doomed, attempts to make our paper airplanes fly and our construction of the puppet show plane-crash, which involved lots of playful trying out and discarding of possible movements and props. In the end, the puppet show and its aftermath (stomping on the plane) were called out by audience members as one of the most vivid images of the Composition pieces performed that day.

Finally, the episode illustrates the importance of accepting your collaborators' "offers" and finding ways to disagree that are fruitful for the group's process and product. Dorothy's idea about a boy sliding into home base, which she offered in the first moments of our collaboration, didn't strike me as a particularly good one for our initiating question, and I sensed others might have felt the same way. Rather than dismiss it, however, we agreed to "play with it," responding to it with complementary offers, like the game of catch, then the fans' reactions, and so on.

Ultimately, by individually and collectively saying, "Yes, and . . ." rather than, "I have a better idea," we were strengthened in our capacity to make our composition. In fact, Dorothy's idea "launched something," in the same way an article in that day's paper or a story might have for August Wilson and Todd Kreidler at Cupa Cupa or wherever "the spot" was that day.

~

The collective creation of new work in the theatre arts requires deliberate attention to three interrelated elements:

- the materials artists draw on, both *inner*, or representational, materials and the more concrete *outer* materials
- the structures, tools, and roles that supply the means for creation
- the modes of engaging with one another and the work, especially inquiry, serious play, and "Yes, and. . . ."

In the next chapter, these same three elements migrate from the rehearsal studios and black box theatre spaces to sites for teacher learning in schools.

4

Collective Creation in the Teachers Room

> A couple of years ago I switched with Katy and did an art lesson, and she did a writing lesson, which was a big joke because I don't do art at all. But I thought that was interesting. Now you don't even think about doing things like that—but why not?"

That's Devin, a fifth-grade language arts teacher at Cooper Elementary School, telling a story to colleagues in his teacher inquiry group—the group we met in chapter 1, one I got to know well over the three years I served as its cofacilitator and documenter. This chapter offers three episodes from the group's first and second year of meeting together. For each, the framework for collective creation (means, materials, modes of engagement) is applied to investigate how the group's activity supports participants' learning and instructional improvement.

Using the framework also surfaces possibilities for how a group's learning might be deepened through attention to the means, materials, and modes of engagement of its collective activity. While the focus in this chapter is the interactions within individual meetings, taken together, the episodes provide images of how a teacher learning group's (TLG's) interactions change over time, a subject explored in more detail in chapter 5.

A TLG AT WORK

The group portrayed in this chapter is the first of three such groups formed at Cooper Elementary School as part of the Evidence Project, a partnership with the Project Zero (PZ) research center at the Harvard Graduate School of Education. The purpose of the project was to develop lessons about and tools for teacher collaboration. As a member of the PZ project team, I worked with all three groups to support their inquiry processes and to document what we were learning about collaboration and teacher learning.

Cooper Elementary School is located in a large Northeastern city, perched on the edge of the dilapidated downtown. It serves an ethnically diverse and economically disadvantaged student population representative of the city as a whole. At the time the partnership with PZ began, administrators and teachers were looking for ways to support students' writing development more effectively, responding to new state tests that included a writing task.

The first "evidence group" was made up of five fourth- to sixth-grade teachers. It met twice a month, once during the school's regularly scheduled professional development meetings after school and once during the school day, using "release time" the principal arranged for participating teachers. Participation in the group was voluntary; however, it satisfied the staff development requirement for those teachers who chose to join the group.

In early meetings during the first year, I introduced the group to an inquiry cycle developed by the PZ team (figure 4.1). We dubbed it the "gears diagram" because it was meant to represent how a group's activities meshed over time to move instructional practice and student learning. As called for by the cycle, I asked teachers to think about the questions they would like to pursue through the group's work. The guidelines for questions specified that they be: (1) important to the individual teacher; (2) of interest to other teachers in the group; and (3) clearly related to student learning.

Most of the teachers' individual questions (see table 4.1) related to students' writing, doubtless influenced by the state tests. As a group, we decided to frame an "umbrella question" to unite these individual interests: "How do we help students become better writers across the curriculum?" Over the course of the year, the group explored the individual and common questions by gathering "evidence" from the teachers' classrooms and using the evidence to address the teachers' questions. The primary forms of evidence teachers gathered and shared were samples of student work, writing prompts and

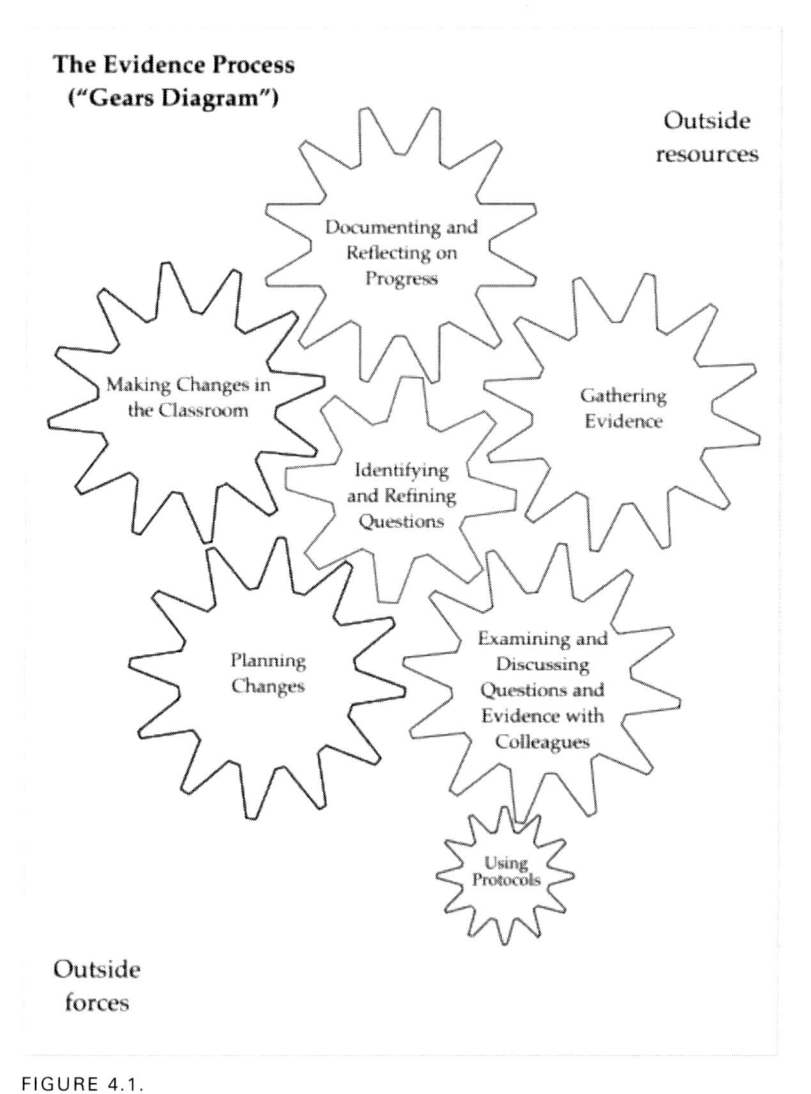

FIGURE 4.1.
The Evidence Process. Project Zero, Harvard Graduate School of Education. Used with permission.

Table 4.1. Teachers' Initial Inquiry Questions

Teacher	*Grade*	*Initial Inquiry Question*
Nora (teacher facilitator)	5th grade	How can I help my students become better at self-editing?
Toni	5th grade	How will my students make the transition from being confident learners/writers to confident speakers?
Devin	5th grade	Am I talking too much?
Lynn	6th grade	How can I be sure everyone understands my directions?
Luis	4th grade	Will my students be ready with the essay portion of [the state assessment]?

assessment instruments created by teachers, and observations of students at work.

The group used several protocols to guide their discussions. At the point described in the first episode that follows, the group had mainly used the Considering Evidence Protocol, developed by the PZ team. It was more often referred to as the "mini protocol" because it had fewer steps than other protocols and was intended to be a relatively quick way to check in on an individual teacher's question and evidence. The steps of the protocol are:

1. Presenter reminds group of his/her inquiry question and briefly describes evidence.
2. Presenter reflects on what evidence may tell him/her about the inquiry question.
3. Full group (including presenter) reflects on what evidence may tell them about the inquiry question.

Initially, I facilitated most of the protocol-guided discussions; over the course of the year, Nora, the group's designated "teacher facilitator," took over much of the facilitation, including the meeting described in the next section.

EPISODE ONE: GENERATING AN INSTRUCTIONAL STRATEGY

This vignette comes from a February meeting from the group's first year. About a month before, the group had discussed students' results on the previous spring's state writing assessment, focusing on those areas in which many students had struggled. They decided to administer a common writing task in all their classes, a compare-contrast essay based on two short reading passages about fantasy stories, and to bring samples of the students' writing to the next meeting. In order to see how students would perform under test-like conditions, they agreed to provide students no instructional support beyond giving the directions to the task.

In the discussion, the group generates a strategy for supporting their students' writing. In the section that follows the vignette, the framework for collective creation is used to investigate how the group's interaction created opportunities for learning about writing and teaching writing—and to propose ways that the learning might be deepened.

"Throw Some of These In. . . ."

Nora began the discussion by inviting her colleagues to "talk about anything that struck you while you did this and observations you made, anything that surprised you, disappointed you. Positive things you saw your kids doing or negative things."

She offered her own observations, noting how quickly students finished the assignment—"I had some kids finished in fifteen minutes." She acknowledged making the mistake of adding to the directions: "I told them to do more. I wish I hadn't done that, just let them do what they were doing."

Lynn told the group she was "really amazed" to see so many of her students completing Venn diagrams rather than writing paragraphs. "It's kind of discouraging because we work on writing paragraphs, writing essays. But I don't really think the directions are clear; nowhere did it say write an essay. . . . It didn't say anything about complete sentences, so I didn't say anything."

Lynn's comment set off a discussion about whether students understood what was expected of them. Lynn gave students lined paper but "still got back graphic organizers. I expected essay. But if you don't say it, how do they know?"

Toni described how she had "revisited" the assignment with her fifth-grade bilingual students, recounting for the group some of her dialogue with students: "I brought it back and said, 'What did you think about that?' They said, 'Oh, that was horrible.' And I said, 'What would have helped?' They said, 'I didn't know if we could put that on paper, or [if] that's what you wanted.'" She talked about one girl's work: "I didn't get anything. I had one organizer and that's it, that's it. And then she tried to write a bit. They had 30 minutes, too, and I only read the directions."

Devin told the group about one student who didn't write anything, and, when he asked him why, replied, "I'm still reading." Devin read from another boy's writing: "I think the two [reading passages] were dumb because they were so fake. 'The One-Eyed Monster' [one of the passages] was probably the worst story I ever read in my life."

Luis: "My students spent two minutes making sure their Venn diagrams were perfect circles. They erased three or four times." He added, "Half of my students, their heads were down, closed their eyes, they just didn't want to deal with this."

Teachers began to offer possible explanations for the students' response to the task. Toni said, "Everything's so creative now. We're trying to be creative. . . . This is more concrete, you need to pull out detail, pull out specifics, go back to the readings."

Lynn: "This is not the way we teach, and I would be surprised if there's any elementary teacher who gives such vague directions and expects at least a two-paragraph essay out of it."

Devin: "I think doing this example is going to change how I teach."

Toni showed surprise at Devin's statement: "But is that always the right way? You're like, 'I have to change how I'm teaching [because] they're not passing the test.' But, you know what, Devin, what if your way is the right way? Just because . . ."

Devin cut her off: "What I mean is every week. . . ."

Luis: "Just throw some of these in there."

Devin: "Just throw more of these in because obviously . . ."

Lynn: "You mean more compare-contrast?"

Devin: "No, more unassisted [writing prompts]. . . . First thing tomorrow morning, I'm taking this out and we're going to go through this and we're going to talk and then I'm going to pull out the [state test] and say, 'Let's look at examples [of writing prompts]' I think it's great. We would have never done this. This was good."

Nora: "I agree, totally agree."

Lynn said, "I'd like to continue to work with these," and Luis responded, "I want to do that."

Reflecting on the Episode

In their discussion, the group addresses important questions about students' writing and how it is assessed. Using the framework for collective creation and bringing in examples from theatre arts practices allows us to see how the group used tools and engaged with materials of different kinds to address the questions. It also reveals some of the ways the group's process might have been more effective in supporting teachers' learning, especially in its mode of engagement.

For this first vignette, each of the elements of the framework is treated separately as a way of demonstrating their usefulness in analyzing activity within TLGs. However, as described in chapter 3, the elements continually overlap and interact with one another.

Means

The vignette offers examples of structure, tools, and roles, the key components of means of collective creation. To begin with structure, the group's work over time is guided by an inquiry cycle, the Evidence Process (figure 4.1), that specifies steps for their inquiry process, from identifying inquiry questions to formulating changes in classroom instruction. In this episode, the group's activity models the stage in the cycle described as: "Examining and discussing questions and evidence with colleagues." As in Bogart or Noon's methods, the group's inquiry process has been initiated by a question, in this case, the group's "umbrella" question, "How can we support students' writing across the curriculum?"

To guide its discussion, the group employs a discussion protocol. While there is no explicit reference to the protocol or its steps, the group's familiarity with the tool is evident from the facilitator's initial invitation to share evidence; the turn taking, in which each teacher presents his or her observations about how students completed the unassisted writing task; and the discussion of implication for the group's question. The implicit protocol here models the steps of the Considering Evidence Protocol ("mini protocol") that the group had been using; here all teachers presented their own evidence and reflected on what it said to them.

Like the scores within the RSVP Cycles, the protocol here functions as a "guide for the realization of objectives" (Halprin & Burns, 1974, p. 32). Also like a score, the protocol may be open or closed. An open score facilitates communication among participants and helps to maintain focus on the question or theme for inquiry but does not determine the outcome of the group's activity; to do so defeats the very purpose of inquiry and collective creation. The protocol here is intended to be open in that it does not specify a particular product, for example, a specific instructional strategy, assessment instrument, or analytical framework.

In facilitating the discussion, Nora enacts the role by inviting her colleagues to "talk about anything that struck you while you did this and observations you made, anything that surprised you, disappointed you." She models a response to the invitation with her own observations about her students' body language during the writing task.

Like Fiona Shaw's question to her acting students about a just-completed improvisation, "What does it do that it's so good?" or Quinn Bauriedel's question to observers of a Composition exercise, "What arrests you?" (see chapter 3), Nora's question elicits reactions that are both specific and emotionally resonant to the individual who offers them.

The framework's inclusion of role as a key component of means provokes us to ask, where might facilitation have made a difference? One such moment is Toni's question for Devin, "What if your way [of teaching writing] is the right way?" By this time, the group was familiar with Devin's approach to teaching writing, which involved discussions with students about his expectations before they actually began to write. Toni's question, thus, appears to name an emerging tension between how they teach students to write and how students' writing is assessed on state tests. In fact, no one responded to Toni's question, and the discussion proceeded to the rapid articulation of an instructional strategy, that is, incorporating similar "unassisted" writing prompts into the teachers' instruction.

Here Nora might have done what directors of theatre companies engaged in collective creation do as a matter of course, that is, to identify or highlight a moment from a performance that might be used somehow within the developing piece (or within a future piece). Sometimes the director simply chooses to note the moment, perhaps to discuss with the actors later; at other times, the director will call attention to it in the moment—as the director of an Open Canvas activity used by the Pig Iron Theatre Company might call out, "Everybody off except the two dancers" (see chapter 3). In either case, the director must be highly attentive to the activity within the group. This "high level of alertness [and] responsiveness" (Bogart, 2001, p. 111) allows him or her to identify such moments in real time and deploy them within the company's ongoing creation process.

Materials

The episode also reveals some of the materials that are often present in TLG meetings. As in the collective creation processes of theatre artists, both *outer* (concrete, observable) materials and *inner* (ideational, representational) materials are evident here. The physical samples of student writing from the unassisted writing prompt and the prompt itself furnish the outer materials. Teachers make explicit reference to these materials, for example, when Devin reads aloud an excerpt from one student's paper ("I think the two passages were dumb because they were so fake"), or when Luis offers a breakdown of how many students had completed Venn diagrams versus those who had written a paragraph or more.

The writing samples are complemented by inner materials, including observations of students at work on the prompt, for instance, Nora's observation about how quickly students finished the task ("I had some kids finished in 15 minutes") or Luis's comment about students' physical behavior ("Half of my students, their heads were down, closed their eyes, they just didn't want to deal with this"). Teachers recount, or replay, interactions they had with their students during the task or discussions with students after they had completed the task. For instance, Toni shares student responses from a discussion in which she asked students what would have helped them to respond to the writing prompt.

Inseparable from the observations and instructional replays (Horn, 2010) are teachers' emotional responses to the students' performances, elicited by Nora's initial invitation to her colleagues to "talk about anything that struck you while you did this and observations you made, anything that surprised you, disappointed you." This facilitation move recalls some of the ways theatre artists generate materials they might then use within their creation processes; for instance, Charles Mee's charge to his collaborators in creating *Hotel Cassiopeia* to make lists of what they "get" from Joseph Cornell's work.

The teachers, too, are including in their discussion what they get from the students' physical writing samples, as well as from their observations of students at work on the task and discussions with students after it. The teachers do not dismiss these observations and emotions as "subjective" or "soft" data. Instead, these inner materials provide the teachers ways to interpret the contents of the student work samples, for example, as they consider how many students completed Venn diagrams rather than the essay the prompt called for (Lynn: "I was amazed").

Using the framework for collective creation could encourage the group to more fully exploit the mix of inner and outer materials within their discussion to generate possibilities that relate to its guiding question. Generating tools, like Mee's "take two from column A and one from column B" technique with the Cornell lists, highlight relationships to explore. The inquiry group might make a similarly deliberate choice to explore relationships between students' verbalized responses to the task (from observations and discussions with students later) and specific elements identified within the writing samples themselves, for instance, students' use of Venn diagrams. To do so depends not only on the variety of materials available but, as discussed above, also on facilitation that actively identifies and highlights possibilities. It also relates to the group's modes of engagement.

Modes of Engagement

The group's activity initially suggests a venting of frustration with their students' performances on the task. However, as teachers begin to offer possibilities for understanding the students' performances, the mode shifts to one that seeks explanations, for example, when Toni offers: "We're trying to be creative [in our instruction]. . . . This is more concrete, you need to pull out detail, pull out specifics, go back to the readings." Or when Lynn states: "This is not the way we teach, and I would be surprised if there's any elementary teacher who gives such vague directions and expects at least a two-paragraph essay out of it."

Here, as well, are glimmers of the "lateral thinking" in Bogart's methods, that is, "freely associating off one another's ideas . . . and [generating] new and exciting ideas about what might happen" (Bogart & Landau, 2005, p. 156). The identification of a tension between writing as tested and writing as taught, articulated first by Lynn in the statement above, is an example of how lateral thinking generates a fruitful idea for further exploration, one that might contribute to the creation of instructional or conceptual resources for individuals and the group.

Almost immediately, however, the mode shifts from lateral thinking to problem solving, as Devin offered a declaration about changing his instructional practice: "I think doing this [using unassisted writing prompt] is going to change how I teach." Toni asks, "What if your way is the right way?" but receives no response from Devin or anyone in the group. Devin's statement that he will change the way he teaches writing is immediately elaborated by Luis through his phrase "throw some of these in there" (meaning writing tasks that reflect the state test), which Devin and Lynn in turn pick up on. Most teachers in the group signal their approval of Devin's idea of including unassisted writing prompts within his instruction; Toni, however, is silent.

The strategy of incorporating ("throw[ing] in") unassisted writing prompts into their classroom instruction certainly represents a product, that is, an instructional strategy that clearly relates to the group's umbrella question. However, the mode of engagement modeled in the latter part of the episode differs from the "Yes, and . . ." mode of theatre artists engaged in collective creation, in which one performer responds to a collaborator's "offer" with neither "yes" nor "no," but rather, "Yes, I will include your suggestion, but I will come at it from another angle and add these new notions" (Bogart, 2001, pp. 88–89). Participants understand that, through this complementary activity, they are not just solving a problem but rather generating a performance that integrates the ideas and input of the entire group.

It is impossible to know how the group's discussion would have been different had it modeled a mode of "Yes, and . . . ," for instance, had it addressed Toni's question about whether Devin's way of teaching writing was the right way. It is reasonable, though, to speculate that a more extended exploration of the tension between methods of teaching writing might have led to other kinds of products, perhaps one that reflected and supported students in identifying multiple purposes and audiences for writing.

To deliberately hold off on solving a problem once it is identified in order to maximize lateral thinking or exploration will feel unnatural and perhaps even counterproductive to most TLGs. But that is, in an important sense, what theatre artists do with tools for source work and lateral thinking: resisting resolution, *for the moment*, and maximizing the generation and exploration of possibilities. The episodes that follow reveal how activity within the group from Cooper develops in ways that are increasingly reflective of this mode of engagement.

EPISODE TWO: PRODUCING AN ANALYTICAL CATEGORY

As the year went on, Nora took on more of the facilitation responsibility. In this April meeting, she facilitates as Lynn presents evidence related to her inquiry question. The group uses a protocol that was relatively new to them, the Modified Collaborative Assessment Conference, referred to by the group as the "in-depth protocol." The protocol is an adaptation of the Collaborative Assessment Conference, developed by Steve Seidel (1998) and colleagues at Project Zero.

In contrast to the Considering Evidence Protocol ("mini protocol"), this one begins with participants describing the "evidence" the presenter has brought and then naming questions the evidence has provoked for them. They do this without any input or response from the presenting teacher. Only after the other participants have described the materials presented and posed questions does the presenter speak again in the discussion. These steps are intended to prevent the natural temptation to evaluate the students' work or air assumptions about the student or the assignment. The steps of protocol are as follows:

1. Presenter reminds group of inquiry question.
2. Participants offer specific descriptions of the evidence (presenter is silent).
3. Participants pose questions the evidence raises for them (presenter is silent).
4. Presenter reflects on descriptions and questions.
5. Entire group discusses how the evidence addresses presenter's inquiry question.
6. Entire group discusses other evidence that might help address inquiry question.

Following the last step, the facilitator typically asks all participants to reflect on how the discussion has supported their learning and to share any other observations or questions about the process.

My colleague and director of the Evidence Project, Steve Seidel, joined the group for this meeting. The episode is divided into two parts; the first focuses on the use of the protocol, the second represents a reflection on the use of the protocol. It is during the reflection that a suggestion from Steve spurs a change in the protocol and its product.

"This One Is for Jackie. . . ."

At the prompting of Nora, Lynn reminded the group of her question: "How do you foster independence and teach at the same time?" She added two questions: "And is everyone understanding? Do I give too much or not enough?" She passed out copies of her evidence: a sample of one student's writing about her mother illustrated with hearts drawn with colored pencils and markers.

Nora asked for descriptions of the evidence.

Devin responded, "She knows when to start new paragraphs."

Nora: "Looks like the assignment was obviously to write about a personal hero. This girl has two, her mom and dad. . . . She seems to be very observant or mature in her observations of her parents."

Toni: "How many children do you know when they're ten [know that] their parents drink and smoke?"

Devin: "Seems like her mother overcame a lot to be a good parent."

Steve: "The combination of the neatness, the hearts, and the amount of feeling described, [and] the sense of pride, makes it a very loving piece."

Nora: "When she makes a statement, she backs it up with examples."

Luis asked, "I was just wondering if the assignment was writing about a personal hero or just writing about heroes in general, and this student decided to make it personal."

Nora invited Lynn to rejoin the conversation, as called for by the protocol. Lynn told the group that the assignment had specifically called for writing about a personal hero.

Other teachers suggested that "personal writing" seemed to elicit more from students than other types of writing. Nora pointed out: "One of the things we've been finding through the reading we're doing [in a teacher researcher course she was taking], and Lynn's evidence, obviously, [is] that when they write something personal . . . how much more you get from them than if it's, 'Write about a starfish,' you know, something that's colder."

I asked Lynn: "Would you say this piece shows more independence than something less personal?"

Lynn: "I'd say more independence, more of who she really is. I think the other ones are *my* assignments, they're for me and this one is for Jackie [the student], for mom and dad. I think that takes the focus off, 'What does Mrs. E. [the teacher] want, versus what do I [the student] want, what am I trying to say?' There is no right way to do this essay."

Lynn referred to another writing assignment she had given students: If You Could Bring Anyone Back to Life. . . . "One girl chose Julius Caesar. The majority chose friends or family members. How can that be wrong?"

Devin: "Did she back it up?"

Lynn: "She did. She knew so much about [Caesar] because that's who she was doing her research project on, and Julius Caesar was fascinating to her at that time."

Reflecting on the Episode, Part I

As in the first episode, this one provides vivid images of means, materials, and modes of engagement present within the group's activity. In relation to *means*, it again reveals the presence of a teacher's inquiry question and the use of a protocol as tools to initiate and guide discussion, and again Nora facilitates the discussion. A key difference in means from the previous episode is that the group uses a different protocol, the Modified Collaborative Assessment Conference, which calls for other participants to describe the "evidence" the presenter shares and name questions the evidence provokes for them before hearing from the presenter about why she chose this evidence to present in relation to her question.

Once again a variety of *materials* is evident. Prominent among these is the physical sample of one child's work, an illustrated piece of writing, written in response to Lynn's assignment to write about a personal hero. The piece provides an important outer-material touchstone for the group's discussion. The descriptions and questions Lynn's colleagues offer, as called for by the protocol, prompt her to bring in inner materials, including her replays of students' responses to other writing assignments she has given, especially one girl's choice of Julius Caesar as the person she would "bring back to life."

The group's initial *mode of engagement* is descriptive and speculative, with teachers offering ideas about what the assignment might have been (for instance, Nora: "Looks like the assignment was obviously to write about a personal hero"). This mode is cued by the protocol steps, which ask the presenting teacher to initially withhold the context for the evidence presented, including the assignment and information about the student(s).

As in the theatre arts practices for collective creation, the protocol-as-tool here encourages the exploration of the materials and generation of new possibilities, which themselves become materials to explore and employ. My question to Lynn about whether Jackie's piece demonstrated more independence than "something less personal" prompts her to identify a difference between pieces of writing that are "my assignments" as opposed to those that are "for

Jackie, for mom and dad." And Luis's question about whether students were asked to write about "a personal hero or just writing about heroes in general," initiates a more extended exploratory discussion than in the first episode, in particular, of different kinds of writing students produce in relation to the different assignments teachers give them. As Nora observes: "when they write something personal . . . how much more you get from them than if it's, 'Write about a starfish,' you know, something that's colder."

At this point in the discussion, the mode of engagement is mainly exploratory. There is little expectation evident for identifying a concrete instructional strategy, as emerged in the previous episode. In the second part of the episode, this absence of a definable outcome raises concerns.

"Just Because It's Personal"

After Nora had closed the discussion, I asked the group to reflect on our process, and, in particular, on our use of the Modified Collaborative Assessment Protocol.

Devin said that he found the step that called for descriptions challenging. Other teachers appreciated how the protocol seemed to both keep the conversation focused and generate new questions and ideas to explore.

Nora agreed, then commented: "I do like that it keeps you focused. It makes you look at one piece and be very observant. I do like that you have to get the questions out there. But I feel like it's hanging. That's the way our discussions have been going this whole time. You don't necessarily resolve all the questions."

Responding to Nora's concern, Steve Seidel suggested that it might be possible for the group to "come to a pretty carefully articulated statement of the one question or the couple of most important questions or conundrums or ideas that come out of the conversation."

Nora replied, "One thing I think, and correct me if I'm wrong, but we all agree that when a student writes about something personal, that's when you see depth and length, that their heart and soul is put into it."

Luis: "Something personal or something also that they're interested in."

Nora: "Right, [it] doesn't necessarily have to be . . ."

Luis: "Just because it's personal . . ."

Nora: "Right, Julius Caesar was enough to spark that girl's [interest]. . . ."

Luis: "Right, it's got to be a little bit of both."

Steve told the teachers that he thought they had identified "a really important modification: something you're interested in. Because you also want to be writing about things in the world that you don't necessarily know or aren't really close but fascinate you and get you going."

Nora described a project her student teacher was doing that involved studying a refugee crisis and organizing a food and money drive for the refugees. "To see the writing they're doing, persuasive letters to parents, they're so interested. I agree completely that it doesn't just have to be something personal."

Reflecting on the Episode, Part II

In reflecting on the discussion of Lynn's evidence and question, Nora shared a frustration that the discussions are "hanging" and do not necessarily resolve the teachers' inquiry questions. Steve's response, that that the group might articulate a question or conundrum that has emerged in the discussion, asks the group to identify and highlight one element from its discussion that might become material for further development.

Identification and selection are essential activities for collective creation in the theatre arts. For example, in the Composition exercise recounted in chapter 3, one member of my group proposed an image of a baseball player sliding into home. The group's decision to select this as a starting point was an important step in creating the composition we ultimately performed—even though we did not actually use the suggested image in the piece we performed. Selecting an idea or image to work with, after a period of exploration or "lateral thinking," does not mean that it will be the final product; however, absent selection, there are too many possibilities to explore—hence, no possibility to advance creation.

This brief episode also provides an image of the theatrical mode of "Yes, and . . ." in action. In the first episode, apart from Toni's unanswered question about "the right way" to teach writing, there was little questioning of Devin's idea of "throwing in" unassisted writing prompts. The idea was accepted by the group more or less as he presented it. Here, in contrast, is the active elaboration of an idea proposed by one member of the group. Nora's naming of a category for student writing, "when a student writes about something personal," is expanded on by Luis: "Something personal or something also that they're interested in." Nora then recalls the girl in Lynn's class who wrote about Julius Caesar because he somehow "spark[ed] that girl's interest." Luis offers a modification: "It's got to be a little bit of both," that is, personal and of interest to the student.

It is still mainly the activity of two people, Nora and Luis, but it does provide an image of "Yes, and. . . ." Nora's original "offer"—to use a term from improv—is accepted and elaborated on and, in the process, transformed into a resource that integrates some of the ideas that have been explored during the meeting (and in prior meetings). The analytical category of writing that is "personal and of interest to the student" will be applied as a conceptual resource within future meetings of the group—and within teachers' individual planning for instruction.

There is another way in which this episode reflects theater arts practices. Recall the Collaboration class in the introduction: Anne Bogart offers her students images for how time progresses in their scene, an aria, and a scene from a film. She does not tell them how to solve the problem; rather she offers them what the Halprins would call a "score" (one element of the RSVP Cycles) to facilitate their working out of the problem.

Steve proposes just such a score to respond to Nora's (and likely others') frustration with the lack of a more clear-cut outcome to the discussion, that is, to formulate a "pretty carefully articulated statement of the one question or the couple of most important questions or conundrums or ideas that come out of the conversation."

It is, in fact, a score for "valuaction," that element of the RSVP Cycles that identifies specific elements of a performance that may contribute to the ongoing development of a piece. Using it allows the group to identify a useful analytical category for student writing. It also influences a change in the protocol (and one we'll see implemented in the next episode), appending a step that asks the group to "identify, highlight, or select a question or idea it might continue to work on."

While there are scores that theatre arts companies use over and over, there are times the director (or someone else in the company) must propose a score to address the situation as it unfolds. The same holds true for the facilitator of a TLG. This relates to the larger challenge for both directors and facilitators of TLGs: to balance robust exploration and generation of possibilities with identification and selection so that collective creation can proceed.

We will return to these challenges in reflecting on the third episode and in chapter 6, where the role of the facilitator in a TLG is related to that of the director in a theatre arts company engaged in collective creation.

EPISODE 3: PROCESS AS PRODUCT

The group at Cooper continued meeting for a second year with one change in membership: Toni had taken a job at another school in the district. The remaining four members continued to meet as a group, and a second group was formed. The original group decided in their first meeting that they would continue to focus on supporting students' writing across the curriculum, and some teachers (including Devin) framed new individual inquiry questions.

In the vignette that follows, many of the features of TLGs identified in the earlier episodes are present, including focus on an inquiry question, a protocol, and facilitation as components of means. The episode illustrates how a tool, or score, created earlier in the group's history, the new final step to the Modified Collaborative Assessment Protocol (described in the previous episode), is applied in support of the group's learning and instructional improvement. As with the previous one, the episode is divided into sections, each with its own analysis.

"I Wanted More than This. . . ."

Since Nora had just facilitated a discussion of another teacher's question and evidence, I agreed to facilitate this one, which focused on Devin's new question: "How can I use a writer's notebook to help my students improve their writing?"

As he passed out copies of one student's writing from a blue examination booklet, Devin began to tell the group that the evidence was a reader's journal entry written in response to the book *From the Mixed-Up Files of Mrs. Basil E. Frankweiler* (Konigsburg, 1967). Nora cut him off: "Too much information!"—a reminder of this protocol's guideline that the presenter does not provide context on the assignment or the student at the outset.

I asked the group to "take a few minutes to review the evidence individually and then we'll start with descriptions." Still pushing lightly against the protocol's constraints, Devin interjected: "I'd be curious if you noticed anything about the student. That's a hint."

Luis: "I see a couple extra pages of *Rascal* [novel] at the end?"

Lynn: "I see predictions."

I asked, "Can you take us to one?"

Lynn quoted from the student's writing: "The first thing I predict: there's to be a very important case . . . Mrs. Basil E. Frankweiler." She added, "So I'm assuming that was before they read the book, maybe looking at the title and the cover?"

Nora: "The person seems to express how, on the second page, he or she feels about what's going on in the book, to have an interaction with what he or she's reading. For example, 'It made me feel funny'; also, 'It made me feel worried.'"

After several more observations, I invited questions that the evidence had provoked. Devin listened silently and took notes.

Nora: "Did the teacher give a format? Was it supposed to be summary, questions, predictions?"

Luis: "Did the teacher look at it after every two or three chapters or just look at it at the end?"

Lynn: "Did you [Devin] have discussion groups before or after they wrote—or at all? If you did, did the 'blue book' [reading journal] enhance the discussions?"

Nora: "Is this typical of how most students responded or is this what you would call an excellent example?"

I said, "In the descriptions, there was a lot of talk about how much writing there is, the kinds of things in the writing. What would you say about the students' enthusiasm for this assignment or series of assignments?"

Lynn: "Going off that, when you said 'take out your blue book,' did you get moans and groans or were they interested in writing after they read?"

Nora: "What were your expectations using this journal and did they [students' performances] match your expectations?"

After a few more questions, I asked Devin to talk about why he brought this piece of evidence and to address some of the questions the group had posed. He told us that he wanted to get a "baseline" on the students' writing in response to the books they read. For that reason, he didn't give them a format, per se, but rather some suggestions. "For example, I wanted a summary, asking yourself questions about the story, and also I wanted them to put themselves in the character if they could."

Devin went on to say that the student whose work we had looked at "came the closest to doing that."

> What was I expecting? I was hoping for this [but] even more so. . . . I don't think any of the kids did enough putting themselves [into it]. You know these kids [in the novel] ran away for three weeks and I wanted to hear them talk about if this was them, what do you think your parents would be going through? And I didn't hear that enough when I read these, and I'm expecting to hear that in *Rascal* [the next book students would read].

He pointed to the part of the student's journal Luis had identified earlier:

> And I really liked the way he started *Rascal* now. He [wrote] about "We learned right away that his mother died" and his father basically lets him do whatever he wants to do and he said "I'd really like that but I wouldn't want to not have a mom." These were great things. So that's it.

Reflecting on the Episode, Part I

The use of the Modified Collaborative Assessment Conference ("in-depth protocol"), as well as the facilitator's questions, encourages a range of descriptions of the student writing sample Devin has presented as evidence, pointing to specific elements of the student's writing, including predictions and emotional responses ("feel worried"). The teachers' questions extend the exploration of the paper, particularly in terms of Devin's expectations for the students' writing in this piece. By the end of this part of the discussion, though, it is not clear that any of this has moved Devin's thinking about his question. He reaffirms his dissatisfaction with students' capacity to "put themselves [into]" their writing in response to the text. No identifiable instructional or conceptual resource is created, at least not in the first part of the group's discussion of Devin's question and evidence.

"Experiment with *Rascal*"

I reminded the group of the additional step to the protocol we'd adopted during the meeting with Steve Seidel in the spring. Turning to Devin, I asked, "Was there anything in the descriptions you heard or any particular question that you think maybe has more relevance for you that we could spend a couple minutes talking about?"

Nora clarified my question, asking, "You mean something he'd like to explore? Anything that stands out for him?"

Devin thought a moment and then said:

> Listening skills maybe. When I look at this, to be honest, two or three kids followed the format all the way through. And so this child obviously internalized what I asked him to do and was able to carry on without any more, or very little, instruction from me. Why were so few able to do that? Don't get me wrong, they did a nice job but not to this degree. . . ."

Devin nodded to Lynn as he referred to her inquiry question:

> And it's kind of fostering independence, like you're looking at. How much should I be giving these kids? Every time we read a chapter, [do] I have to say, "OK, make sure you ask questions, make sure you put yourself in that position"?

Nora suggested Devin make a poster with his expectations for the journal responses. This led Devin to admit that, with fifth graders, "I'm probably going to remind them on a much more consistent basis of what I want them to do. I suppose that's not a bad thing."

Lynn wondered whether using a poster to remind students of expectations "sometimes curbs their creativity because they only answer the three things on the board . . . it's kind of a catch-22." She proposed that Devin "sort of experiment with *Rascal*," that is, "go a couple days without giving students explicit reminders of your expectations."

I asked, "Devin, if you were going to bring more evidence about this question about listening skill and how it varies, how to teach it, what might that evidence be? I guess I'm asking the whole group [to respond to] that."

Devin: "It goes back to my original question [from the previous year], 'Do I talk too much?' Because if I do talk too much, then is some of that, you know. . . . But to answer your question about evidence of listening, I think anything they do on an assignment is listening, so if you look at any work students have, it is evidence."

This prompted more questions about how Devin gave students feedback. As I invited any last thoughts or questions to wrap up, Luis asked:

> What if you gave an example; you put yourself in? "This is what I would do." Maybe do it again next chapter, then sit back and see if they bring it up, and once Johnny [a student] brings it up, you can share with the class. You know how you said you were looking [for] more personal [responses]? He started doing that in *Rascal*, his mother dying. Put yourself in that situation and share with the class, then do it again the next chapter. If you get one student who does, share that with the class.

Devin responded:

> What I tried to do when I read the first chapter of *Rascal*, I said for me it has a lot of childhood memories. I used to go out hunting, walking through the woods when I was a child. I had a lot of independence. I could just go out. My parents wouldn't be worried. You kids don't have that today. And try to relate those personal [responses]. It wasn't the same but that's a good idea: What would *I* do?

Checking the time, I turned to Nora: "I think if we want to stay on schedule . . . sorry to cut this off. Why don't we end this protocol here?"

Reflecting on the Episode, Part II

If I had been thinking of the group's activity as collective creation when I was facilitating this part of the group's meeting, I would not have ended the discussion when I did, even though discussion of another teacher's question and evidence was scheduled and time was running short. Here's why: The group was doing what theatre arts companies engaged in collective creation strive to do: respond to a question, draw on a variety of materials, explore relationships among the materials and the question, and highlight the possibilities that emerge as materials with which to compose products that may be used in their ongoing work.

For theatre arts companies, these products are performances, which are applied, for example, within a new round of Composition exercises (see chapter 3) or in developing the play script. In TLGs, two broad categories for products exist: instructional resources and conceptual resources. The former are strategies or tools that can be used by teachers in their classrooms; the latter are inquiry questions, analytical categories or frameworks, and other "thought resources" that can be used within the group's continued collective creation.

The first episode provided an example of an instructional resource: Devin's idea for "throwing in" unassisted writing prompts to his teaching. This episode reveals the possible inception of another instructional strategy when Luis proposes that Devin "put [himself] in that situation and share with the class"; in other words, model for students his own personal response to the book they are reading. What makes this instructional resource more robust than the earlier one is the way it integrates materials from the group's discussion, especially Lynn's proposal that Devin "experiment with *Rascal*," that is, provide explicit reminders of his expectations for students' written responses to the reading, then see what happens when he doesn't provide them for a few days.

The instructional strategy is itself integrated within a larger conceptual resource the group is composing through its ongoing process, that is, an understanding of teaching and the teacher-student interaction as a kind of experimentation. In fact, it is possible to claim that the group's process is continuous with its product, an experimentation perspective on teaching itself.

Applying the framework for collective creation helps to see how this process-as-product is composed. Devin's question, the protocol, and the facilitation of the discussion are all elements of the means through which the group interacts. The student work sample provides the initial material for the interaction. The descriptions and questions, called for by the protocol, generate additional materials for the group to explore and relate to one another.

For example, questions about Devin's expectations for students' reading journals prompt Devin to expand on what he was looking for in the students' writing ("I don't think any of the kids did enough putting themselves [into it]"). These become materials for an exploration of the catch-22, identified by Lynn, of being explicit with students about expectations and about students developing independence. It is this tension that provokes the idea of treating his approach to introducing a written response to a text as an experiment, or in other words, to see how students pick up on the subtle modeling Devin provides through his talk.

The modes of that engagement are as significant here as the materials or means. The early joking about following the protocol proscription on sharing context information at the start ("Too much information!") establishes a playful mode, as does the nature of the task: describing the evidence without context from the presenting teacher (who could easily provide it), as well as posing questions that aren't immediately answered, suggests a game-playing mode. There is an imaginative and speculative quality to this part of the discussion that energizes the group and, as noted above, generates possibilities with which to compose products—in other words, a mode of "serious play," like that of theatre artists (see chapter 3).

To engage that mode, participants must resist the temptation to jump to a solution, as in the first episode. By doing so, a space opens for exploration of relationships among materials and the presenter's question. When the mode of activity does become more product-oriented—provoked perhaps by the added final step to the protocol—the products composed are likely to be more robust because they derive from a richer set of materials and reflect a more extended exploration of relationships.

If I was facilitating the same discussion now, I hope I would recognize the process-as-product that was developing and propose a score to sustain its development. The goal would be to foster the creation of a product that would truly reflect the richness and complexity of the group's discussion. To do so is to ask, along with Devin in his story about switching places with an art teacher, *why not*? Why not make space for serious play within our professional exchanges? And what is lost by not doing so?

~

The three episodes from the inquiry group at Cooper Elementary School illustrate some of the ways means, materials, and modes of engagement function within a TLG's meetings. They also demonstrate how the interaction of these elements shapes the products of the group's activity. In the first episode, the relative dominance of a problem-solving mode led to the definition of a strategy that mimics the state-mandated writing test. In the later episodes, a greater commitment to exploration of materials and composition of possibilities produced more robust conceptual resources, including an analytical category for students' writing and an appreciation of the group's process as ongoing experimentation.

As we'll see in the next chapter, collective creation takes place not just in meetings like these but also in how a group's activity develops over time.

5

Exquisite Pressure and Cumulative Progression

In the math department office of a small public high school in East Harlem, Suzy Ort, the school's instructional coach, meets with Caitlin, a young math teacher during her prep period.[1]

Suzy: "What's going on?"

Caitlin: "Half my students are failing." She describes for Suzy one student who puts in the work but doesn't get it. "I feel a lot of pressure to give students a 60 [passing grade]."

Suzy: "What about your plan to have students taking over, teaching topics?"

Caitlin: "I brought it up with my students. I reminded them that a big part of their grade would be teaching."

Suzy cautions, "It's probably not the best thing to have students model the kind of instruction you do," explaining that students are unlikely to have the content knowledge necessary to teach the topics, not to speak of the classroom management skills. "You're going to have to set the project up a different way. Produce something."

Caitlin: "Produce a poster?"

Suzy: "A poster or . . . Have I ever showed you my favorite review sheet activity? Students create review sheets." She describes how, in groups, students create handouts for their classmates that cover the key content for the unit. "Get them to do stuff, to do the application of ideas."

Caitlin responds, "This is going to be a disaster." But she has already accepted the idea, and she and Suzy begin to discuss the best way to group students for the activity.

~

This chapter draws on a study of professional development at Park East High School, where Caitlin and Suzy are working, to explore a tension inherent in collective creation, whether it occurs in theatre arts companies or teacher learning groups (TLGs).

On one side of the tension, for a group to become a vehicle for professional learning and instructional improvement, its activity must result in products that integrate and extend participants' learning. For TLGs, I've identified two categories of products: *conceptual* resources, such as inquiry questions and analytical categories for student learning, and *instructional* resources, such as classroom strategies and assessment instruments.

On the other side of the tension, a group's natural impulse to produce something useful can eclipse the potential for learning inherent in the creation process itself—think of, from the Cooper Elementary School group, Devin's unexplored idea of "throwing in" unassisted writing prompts to his instruction. This may be especially true when participants are driven by an immediate need, like Caitlin's, for something to use with her students—maybe even next period!

To address this tension, two more extended episodes from Park East High School are examined: first, a brief planning meeting of the coach with two social studies teachers and then a story of how an interdisciplinary instructional strategy for scaffolding students' analytical and writing skills developed over several years. Once again, methods for collective creation in the theatre arts offer resources for thinking about how teachers' interactions support professional learning and instructional improvement.

The vignettes illustrate how collective creation functions on two timescales, one labeled "exquisite pressure," after Bogart and Landau (2005), and another "cumulative progression," after Dewey (1934). They also reveal how collective creation occurs in different settings. These include more formal group meetings, as with the Cooper Elementary School inquiry group in chapter 4, but also one-on-one and small-group coaching interactions, department meetings, and even informal interactions among colleagues.

Whatever the setting, attention to the means, materials, and modes of engagement helps us to understand how a group's activity contributes to collective creation—and how it might do so more effectively.

Creating Fast and Slow

In his 2011 bestseller, *Thinking, Fast and Slow*, Daniel Kahneman distinguished two systems for thinking:

> System 1 operates automatically and quickly, with little or no effort and no sense of voluntary control. System 2 allocates attention to the effortful mental acts that demand it, including complex computations. The operations of System 2 are often associated with the subjective experience of agency, choice, and concentration. (pp. 20–21)

For Kahneman, both "fast" thinking (system 1) and "slow" thinking (system 2) are beneficial, but for different purposes and in different settings.

That thinking—or creation itself—occurs on different timescales has long been recognized by artists and perhaps most acutely by theatre artists. Faced with way-too-short production schedules and way-too-soon opening nights, how could they not be hyperaware of time and how to use it productively? The response to this familiar situation, of at least some theatre artists, is to embrace two seemingly paradoxical tenets: (1) good work develops only over sustained periods of time and (2) very short periods of time can generate very good work.

Addressing the latter tenet, directors Bogart and Landau (2005) maintain that "when we are not given the time to think or talk too much (because someone has set a time limit), wonderful work often emerges" (p. 138). In other words, to deliberately limit time for collaborating can be an effective means to enable creation; it engenders a mode of engagement that Bogart and Landau term "exquisite pressure."

> Give them just enough time in the Composition assignment to create something they can own and repeat (so it's not just improv and accident), but not so much time they can stop to think or judge even for an instant. It's often useful to say: "You have twenty minutes—go." (p. 139)

The pieces the groups create and perform after twenty (or forty or sixty) minutes of working together (see chapter 3) are indeed complete works that the performers can "own and repeat" (Bogart & Landau, 2005, p. 139). Composition exercises are meant to encourage creation of a performance (as product); however, this is not the primary purpose for Composition exercises. Instead, Composition—and exquisite pressure itself—is intended to generate the "theater vocabulary that will be used for any given piece" (Bogart & Landau, p. 12), in other words, ideas, images, text, and so on, that may become materials in the creation of the piece for performance.

Collective creation calls for a second timescale, one in which the (exquisite) pressure of the clock gives way for a less constrained experience of time, one that allows for the "cumulative progression" Dewey (1934) equated with the creation of a work of art. Cumulative progression encompasses alternating periods of seeking and finding, doing and reflecting, summing and conserving. It involves "managing the richness of ideas" (Rabinow, 2003) that have been generated, often through forms of exquisite pressure: selecting, organizing, adding emphasis, and so on. Cumulative pressure, like Kahneman's system 2, is more deliberate whereas exquisite pressure, like system 1, is more intuitive.

Chapter 3 introduced a tool used by Charles Mee and the SITI Company for generating possibilities to explore in creating the play *Hotel Cassiopeia*. Mee started by creating separate lists of what Joseph Cornell's work made him think of. Then he invited company members to create their own lists; from these, he distilled one list of "ingredients," which he gave to Bogart and her company to use to create Composition pieces.

As he observed the pieces they made, he identified specific moments, which in turn became ingredients in new compositions. Through this process, he developed the script for the play. In fact, even with a script, the company had much composing to do; Mee is known for leaving much to the interpretation of the actors, designers, and director (Cummings, 2006).

The story illustrates how episodes of exquisite pressure (making lists, Composition, Open Canvas activities, etc.) contribute to a more extensive process of cumulative progression. Both systems for collective creation are essential. In the following sections, two more episodes from Park East High School allow us to explore collective creation on these different timescales. The chapter concludes with a look back at the inquiry group from Cooper Elementary School, now applying the dual lenses of exquisite pressure and cumulative progression.

AN EPISODE OF EXQUISITE PRESSURE

Many, if not most, of the professional interactions teachers have are severely constrained by time. Often, they take place between classes or during a lunch break. Even regularly occurring meetings designated as common planning time are likely to be brief, typically forty minutes at most. In the vignette that follows, one such meeting provides an example of exquisite pressure.

From the Bill of Rights to *Black Hawk Down*

Around a table in the small social studies department office, Suzy (the coach) is meeting with Jennie, a teacher in her second year, and Joe, who has taught at the school for five years.

Suzy, opening her notebook: "So, where are you?"

Jennie: "Okay, this is where I am. In Government, we finished forms of government this week and we'll have a test on Thursday. I'll start the Constitution and forms of government next week. I'll start in the U.S. . . . Actually, I'm not really sure how to start."

Suzy: "Do you want to talk about the Bill of Rights? Real-life examples of real-life protections the Bill of Rights provides?"

Joe: "I would push the kids. Pull out a Federalist paper or anti-Federalist tract. Why was the Bill of Rights created? Why it's democratic and the rest of the Constitution is less democratic. Have you done the Social Contract with them?"

Jennie: "No."

Joe, getting up to leave the room: "I have something you might be able to use."

Suzy and Jennie talk about how students responded to *Tombstone,* a movie Jennie had shown her classes.

Joe returns and hands Jennie a copy of his activity. He says, "Basically, the students write a social contract as a group."

Jennie, a bit uncertainly: "Social Contract is basically . . ."

Suzy: "A bargain we make in the world for peace to exist."

Joe: "You give up the state of nature for law to exist."

Jennie: "What would be an example of a rule a group would make up?"

Joe: "One group said Neeta wouldn't chew gum for a week and Dewayne wouldn't curse." Knowing both students, all three laugh.

Jennie: "Alright. Hey, I think it's cool."

Joe: "When you come back to the Declaration of Independence, it makes it more possible for them to understand [it]."

Jennie asks Joe about the sequence of activities and readings he used, taking notes on the back of the activity sheet as he talks.

Suzy: "And you would use the same process when you do the Constitution and Bill of Rights?"

Joe: "I hate the Constitution; it's so dull and difficult. But I love the Bill of Rights."

Suzy disagrees with Joe about the Constitution, but asks: "So just do the Bill of Rights?"

Joe: "I might look at it through the idea of compromise."

Suzy: "Or as a flexible document, something that changes. . . ."

For two or three minutes more, Suzy and Joe share other ways of teaching the Constitution, for example, connecting it to specific court cases.

Suzy: "OK, I'm looking at the clock, just because Jennie is doing current events with the movie theme. Do you think if kids chose their own movie with a political theme, for example, *Black Hawk Down*, it could be an independent project?"

In the brief discussion that follows, Joe shares some strategies he and his co-teacher, Drew, have developed to help students know "how to watch a movie," for example, identifying the elements of a film: setting, characterization, plot, and so on. "We found we needed to watch more films with [the students] for them to get it."

By the time the bell rings, the teachers have gathered their materials and departed for their classes.

Reflecting on the Episode

On the surface, this meeting is similar to the one that began the chapter between Suzy and Caitlin. Again, a less experienced teacher seeks help from more experienced colleagues on an instructional problem: how to introduce specific curricular content. Again, colleagues offer suggestions; here, Joe shares with Jennie a specific activity he has used with his students, much as Suzy shared her review sheet activity with Caitlin.

Applying the framework for collective creation allows us to discern some significant commonalities between episodes in the means for supporting teacher learning and instructional improvement. While Suzy's interactions with the teachers in both meetings feel spontaneous and informal, they follow a pattern, one evident in her meetings with teachers. Suzy's questions typically address four critical elements of planning:

- *Timeline*: What's going on? Where are you (in relation to your goals)? What do you need to accomplish (with your students) by a certain date?
- *Content*: What are you working on (e.g., topics, texts, skills)?
- *Assignments*: How might you introduce that (concept, topic, text, etc.) to students?
- *Products*: What will students produce?

These dimensions comprise a "score," in the language of the RSVP Cycles (see chapter 3), a framework that initiates and guides the group's collaborative activity. It does so by highlighting a focus (Jennie's question about introducing the Constitution) and inviting input, ideas, and objectives from participants (Jennie, Joe, and Suzy).

Also like a theatre artist's score, it is "open": it does not impose a predetermined outcome. It does, however, underline the expectation for a product of some kind addresses the focus (problem of instruction). "Produce something," Suzy tells Caitlin in the earlier episode, and their discussion quickly moves from one possible student-created product, student-taught lessons, to another, the collaborative construction of a review sheet. Similarly, in this vignette, Jennie adapts Joe's social contract activity to use with her students, in which students develop a contract for their own class.

Of course, Suzy is talking about what students produce but the effect is to encourage the teachers' production of something they can actually use. Bogart and Landau expect their actors to produce a Composition piece—something they can "own and repeat"—after just twenty minutes or so of working. In a similarly brief period of time, Suzy expects the teachers to adapt or create an instructional strategy or tool that results in a student product. Exquisite pressure!

The score identified above is an effective means for producing a solution to an immediate problem. It does so by encouraging the generation of multiple possibilities—in this case, for introducing the Constitution—from which to select or adapt for use. At the same time, it limits the potential for collective creation. The expectation for identifying one strategy or tool, and to do so in such a short time period, obscures other possibilities for exploration and, ultimately, constrains collective creation. In this sense, the score may not be open enough; that is, it may not allow for sufficient exploration of possibilities and how they relate to the focus.

As in the early inquiry group meeting at Cooper Elementary School in the last chapter, the rapid-fire development of the strategy for "throwing in" unassisted writing prompts to teachers' instruction bypassed some of the questions generated by examining the student writing samples (and other materials); for instance, how does the way the state assesses student writing relate to the way teachers teach writing? Had the group engaged this question, it might have created a different, and potentially more robust, instructional or conceptual resource, for example, a framework or typology of the purposes for student writing.

In this meeting at Park East, the range of approaches to introducing the Constitution might, for example, contribute to the creation of an inquiry question about what students learn from different approaches (a conceptual resource). Or, explored along with other materials (samples of student work, curriculum standards, etc.), these strategies might be employed in constructing a sequence of activities and assessments to support students' learning about foundational historical documents (an instructional resource).

Speculating about these "ghost products" is not to deny the very real benefits of discussions among colleagues that help to solve an immediate problem or generate a possible teaching strategy. Both Caitlin and Jennie leave their meetings with clearer ideas of how to teach their specific curricular content.

However, such moments, on their own, do not typically result in the creation of resources for instruction and teacher learning that extend beyond an individual teacher's specific need for a specific class; in other words, they do not produce resources that can be used in a range of settings, by a range of teachers, including powerful and flexible instructional strategies, analytical frameworks for students' learning, and inquiry questions that help teachers and their learning groups to investigate critical aspects of learning and instruction.

In the hurly-burly of teachers' school days, it is not surprising that most professional interactions—when they happen at all—do not lead to the creation of such products. It is not the nature of exquisite pressure to do so.

Products such as these demand different means, materials, and modes of engagement than we've seen in the meetings described so far.

A STORY OF CUMULATIVE PROGRESSION

As a temporal dimension of collective creation, cumulative progression is not isolated from exquisite pressure; on the contrary, it frequently relies upon the products of exquisite pressure to succeed. To explore the dynamics of cumulative progression, including its relationship to exquisite pressure, another episode from Park East High School is presented below, one that unfolded over time and involved the coach and teachers from across the school.

Making a Better "BBQ"

I was just about to conclude my first extended interview with Suzy after shadowing her coaching activities for several days, when she asked, "Can I tell you one short story?" How could I refuse? The story she told, and that I investigated through interviews with teachers involved, turned out to be not so short after all. It revealed how a schoolwide instructional practice had been created over several years, as the timeline in figure 5.1 portrays.

Year 1	• Lisa and Drew learn about Joe's DBQ activities. • Lisa and Drew develop initial BBQ for teaching *Animal Farm* in their Humanities classes.
Year 2	• Lisa leaves school. Drew continues to use BBQs. • Drew does a brief presentation on the BBQ during a full-faculty PD session. • Suzy shares BBQs and student writing samples with other teachers. • Some teachers begin to use BBQs in their classes.
Year 3	• Drew leaves. Suzy continues to share BBQ. • Other teachers continue to use in their classes.
Year 4	• Drew returns. Drew and Joe co-teach Humanities classes using BBQs. • Joe and Drew lead a full-faculty session on BBQs.
Year 5 onward	• Teachers continue to use BBQs in their classes • New tools developed by teachers include "MBQ" (Movie Based Questions) and the Document Protocol.

FIGURE 5.1
Timeline of BBQ development.

When Lisa and Drew began teaching a new ninth-grade humanities course integrating English language arts and history, one of their major goals was for students to use evidence from primary source documents in formulating their positions in writing. Most Park East students enter the school with weak analytical and writing skills, and the two teachers felt this would be an important focus for the course.

They learned that their colleague Joe (whom we met earlier) had had some success getting his Global Studies students to answer Document-Based Questions, or "DBQs," a staple of the New York State Regents exams in history. One of Joe's instructional strategies was for students to develop their own questions about the historical documents they studied; in other words, "look at a document; ask a question about it; answer it; put it all together to write a document-based question for the exam."

Lisa and Drew liked Joe's focus on getting students to use evidence from documents in their writing. However, because they were using complete books (for example, *Animal Farm*), they decided that they would create the questions and stagger these across students' reading of the book. Each question would require students to identify and use evidence from a specific section of the book the class had just read. They knew that students tended to produce better work when the teachers' expectations were clear and visible to students, so they developed a one-page instrument (or graphic organizer), which they dubbed a Book-Based Question, or "BBQ," to differentiate from the more familiar DBQs.

Each BBQ would have the same format and sequence: At the top of the document, students are directed to address an "overarching question" about the text. Then students are to identify evidence from the text related to the question, organizing it within a chart with three columns: (1) page number, (2) T, M, B, (for top, middle, bottom of the page, to help students locate the evidence for later use), and (3) Quote/Comments (for relevant quotations from the text and the student's commentary on them). Finally, using the evidence from their chart, students construct two-paragraph responses to the question. (Figure 5.2 provides an example of the format.)

Initially, the BBQs were envisioned as assessments of students' ability to identify evidence from a text in response to a thematic question. As Lisa and Drew saw the kinds of analyses some of the students were now completing, they realized that, collectively, the individual BBQs could help students ad-

Animal Farm BBQ 2: The New Republic

Context: Old Major has described his vision of an ideal farm. Now, the animals begin the process of turning "Manor Farm" into "Animal Farm."

Question: What different actions do the animals perform to support Old Major's ideology of a farm worked and owned by and for animals? Try to find four different actions.
Procedure for BBQs:

1. Read the context and the question.

2. Use the box below to take notes while reading

3. Answer the question in paragraph form on the back of this page. Direct quotes from the novel, along with explanations, are the best types of evidence to use.

(Ex: On page 18, Old Major says, "................" This shows his support for the new farm by....)

Page #	T, M, B	Quote/Comments

Response: What different actions do the animals perform to support Old Major's ideology for the new Animal Farm?

Figure 5.2
Sample Book-Based Question. Drew Allsopp & Joseph Schmidt, Park East High School. Used with permission.

dress more global analyses of the text. They started to design end-of-unit essay assignments so that students could draw on their responses to all of the four or five BBQs they complete while reading the text.

As the teachers read their students' essays, they saw improvements not only in many students' use of evidence but also in their overall writing. They shared their findings with Suzy, the coach, who, in turn, began to share with other teachers samples of the "really good writing" some students were doing. Suzy recalled:

> I start carrying [the student writing samples] in my notebook and every time that people ask me about reading and about students writing about texts, I whip them out. I share them with Clancy (English), I share them with Jennie (social studies), I share them with Brianne (social studies), and I share them with Carrie.

Suzy described how Carrie was able to use the strategy to help her senior English students engage with a challenging book:

> Carrie's class was reading *Rebecca*, a very ambitious text, and she's looking for something to do because the kids don't get it. It's a complicated book—they don't love it—so she's looking for something to do, a way to give them access to the text. And it worked!

Over the next two years, more teachers incorporated BBQs within their instruction. Lisa left the school, and Joe and Drew co-taught the humanities course. Drew and Joe shared a concern with Suzy about how the strategy was being applied by some teachers. As Joe describes it, the purpose of the BBQ was to support students in their ability "to develop arguments in response to larger thematic questions." Instead, some of the BBQs were "too 'facty' and too 'worksheety.'"

Suzy saw an opportunity to address the issue in an upcoming full-faculty professional development meeting. Rather than working within department groups, as had been planned, she proposed Drew and Joe present some of the BBQs they had used with students, for example the one included here as figure 5.2, and talk about "the thinking behind [the BBQ] and how they're done in their classes." The meeting was successful both in expanding interest in the BBQs and also establishing a better understanding of the kinds of textual analyses and writing the strategy supports.

The BBQ continues to be used as an instructional tool in classes across the curriculum. In fact, its effectiveness has spawned the development of other instructional tools, such as Joe and Drew's MBQs (Movie-Based Questions) or the Document Protocol used to scaffold students in analyzing images of all sorts: cartoons, maps, graphs, photographs, and so forth. The latter was developed by Pete, an English teacher who was not even working at the school when the early events in this story took place.

Reflecting on the Story

If this story represents a successful episode of collective creation, then it must result in a product or products: conceptual or instructional resources. Certainly, the BBQ format itself is one product or instructional resource: a tool students can use in identifying evidence from a text they are reading and synthesizing the evidence into a written response to a question about the text.

If the story is viewed on a longer timescale, the outline of another product becomes visible: a schoolwide, cross-disciplinary instructional strategy for scaffolding students' capacities for textual analysis and persuasive writing. What are the means, materials, and modes of engagement that contributed to this conceptual resource?

Means

Episodes of cumulative progression, like those of exquisite pressure, are typically initiated by a question or problem. Here, Drew and Lisa wanted to find a way to get their students to use textual evidence from books they were reading more effectively in their writing. That this problem was not a new discovery or one unique to the two of them does not diminish its pertinence; in fact, it may have made it more likely that their efforts to address it would resonate with other teachers.

Episodes of exquisite pressure, witnessed above in Suzy's interactions with Caitlin and Joe and Jennie, as well as in the meetings of the Cooper Elementary School inquiry group described in chapter 4, respond well to a time limit and the use of a score (a set of questions, a discussion protocol, etc.) to initiate and guide the activity within that time. In the BBQ story, there was no predetermined period of time for the development of the product—indeed, one could argue that it is ongoing in the creation of new tools, such as Pete's Document Protocol. Nor was there an explicit structure or set of steps established in advance to sequence activities.

Cumulative progression instead relies on means that are distributed over time, more responsive, but ultimately no less deliberate than those for exquisite pressure. These include tools for selecting, recording, and deploying materials to encourage the collective creation of resources for teacher learning and instructional improvement, especially those that will have long-lasting influence on teaching and learning across the school.

In collective creation in the theatre arts, there is a rhythm or cycle of generating materials, selecting, and applying, then generating, selecting, applying again, and so on. Specific tools for generating materials include creating lists, free writing, Composition and Open Canvas activities, and many others (see chapter 3). These manifestations of exquisite pressure generate a plethora of material possibilities—images, texts, uses of sound or music, and so forth—most of which will *not* be used. The skillful director is able to select—identify and highlight—from all the possibilities, those that have generative potential for the creation of the piece.

This kind of selection calls for deep understanding of and commitment to the question or problem the company is working on. It also demands an extraordinary degree of attention to the activities of the company. Of course, directors must be able to record these moments as they occur so that they can be recalled and deployed at later stages of the collective creation process.

Most directors maintain a notebook of some kind as they observe performances. Others may rely on a particularly acute visual memory. Katharine Noon, of the Ghost Road Company, insists on transcribing videotapes of Composition pieces and rehearsals so that she (along with other members of the company) can select moments of possibility from a detailed record of prior performances.

Selection, no matter how informed and judicious, means nothing without a way to get the selected material, or moments of possibility, into the company's activity. This deployment might involve including one or more selected materials within the list of ingredients for a new Composition exercise or into the developing script for performance itself.

In an early "Snapshots" (tableaux) activity from the Ghost Road Company workshop (described in chapter 3), one participant used a sheet in a variety of ways. In the next set of compositions, director Katharine asked each group to include the use of a sheet. Groups found different ways to address this required "ingredient." One used a sheet to suggest water overtaking a family fleeing from Hurricane Katrina. This use, in a different context, became part of the script for our final, collective performance.

In the BBQ story, the coach's activity models these same tools. When Suzy heard from Lisa and Drew about students' improved writing using the BBQs, she recognized that this might provide useful possibilities for working with other teachers in supporting more proficient student writing. Her selection of this emerging tool from the strategies teachers were using reflected her own deep involvement with and commitment to improving student writing across disciplines and grade levels, one that had developed through classroom observations and meetings with teachers and administrators.

Recording made a difference, too. Suzy carries a large ring-bound notebook with her at all times. In it she includes notes from meetings with teachers and observations of classes, lists of things she needs to do or wants to talk about with teachers, and artifacts she thinks might be useful. In addition to taking notes during her discussions with Drew and Lisa about the BBQ, she asked for copies of the BBQs and samples of student essays that had shown stronger writing with evidence. That richly detailed record became a crucial resource for encouraging the use of BBQs by other teachers, in other words, deploying the materials.

Of course a school coach, unlike a theatre director, cannot require a teacher to include an "ingredient" in his or her teaching. This challenges coaches and others supporting teachers' learning and instructional improvement to find effective ways to encourage teachers to incorporate potentially generative possibilities into their instruction. There are two specific means through which the BBQ, as an example of such a possibility, was deployed.

Informally and largely one-on-one, Suzy shared the students' writing from Drew and Lisa's essays with other teachers. This approach was effective in getting several other teachers to try similar approaches. Later, and more formally, Suzy asked Joe and Drew to present the BBQ as a tool and discuss its purposes at a whole-faculty professional development session—a manifestation of "valuaction," or critical self-reflection, on the development process. These forms of deployment worked in concert to encourage experimentation with the tool by teachers, elaboration of the strategy, critical reflection on its effective uses, and refinement.

Materials

Previous chapters have illustrated the broad range of materials theatre artists draw upon in their processes of collective creation. The outer (or concrete) materials include texts, images of all kinds, movement, music, and songs. Inner (ideational) materials include participants' memories, imaginations, and even emotional responses related to an initiating question or theme. Materials are identified, generated, explored, selected (or discarded), integrated, and organized through processes of cumulative progression to compose a final product, that is, the script and the performance itself.

What are the materials from which the schoolwide instructional strategy of using BBQs to support students' analysis and writing was composed? Clearly, teacher-created assignments represent a critical form of *outer* materials in this story, especially Joe's DBQ assignments. While Drew and Lisa did not adopt Joe's DBQ approach, the assignments provided a concrete possibility to work with for supporting students' capacity to use evidence from a text. Similarly, the initial BBQs developed by Lisa and Drew that Suzy shared with other teachers offered them models for how they might create tasks for their own classes and students.

Equally important as materials for collective creation were the samples of students' writing that resulted from the BBQs. For teachers struggling to support their students' writing, these provided tangible images of the quality their own students might attain. A reflection of this can be seen in how the inquiry group at Cooper Elementary School responds to student writing samples in creating the analytical category for writing that is personal and interesting to an individual student (see chapter 4).

No matter how impressive these outer materials were on their own, they would be insufficient for the creation of a schoolwide strategy. Achieving that also required *inner* materials, namely, stories. Even before Drew and Lisa saw the specific tasks Joe was giving students or samples of his students' writing, they had heard about the quality of writing his students were doing from Suzy and from Joe himself. The story of Joe's success with teaching students to use evidence from the text in their writing attracted Drew and Lisa's interest to the instructional strategy.

Stories also played a role in disseminating the positive results of Drew and Lisa's initial BBQs. One might call these "illustrated stories"—combining inner and outer materials; in telling other teachers about the successful strategy, Suzy pulled out examples of the BBQs and students' writing. In fact, the very enthusiasm for the teachers' and students' work with which she inflects the telling can be seen as an inner material in its own right—as necessary for cumulative progression as student writing samples or the BBQ instruments themselves—a notion to return to when considering modes of engagement below.

Modes of Engagement

For the earlier episodes, both Suzy's meeting with Caitlin and the discussion of how to introduce the Bill of Rights, the mode was largely problem solving, in particular, generating possible solutions to a specific problem of how to introduce or treat specific curricular content. In the story of the BBQ, the mode is closer to that of composition: a rhythm of doing, selecting, organizing, adding emphasis, and adjusting is evident in the participants' (teachers' and coach's) interactions with each other and in relation to their collective activity.

It is also possible to understand these interactions, across multiple years, as a manifestation of the now-familiar theatre arts mode of "Yes, and . . . ," in which performers commit themselves to accepting and elaborating their collaborators' offers rather than introducing something entirely new or idiosyncratic. As Bogart (2001) points out, operating in this mode does not mean knee-jerk or automatic acceptance of a collaborator's idea or approach, rather it means saying:

> "Yes, I will include your suggestion, but I will come at it from another angle and add these new notions." It means that we attack one another, that we may collide; it means that we may argue, doubt each other, offer alternatives. It means that feisty doubt and a lively atmosphere exist between us. (pp. 88–89)

This mode is integral to the "micropractices" of theatre artists, such as improv and Composition exercises. It is also essential to the creation of performances on longer timescales.

In the BBQ story, this mode is evident in Drew and Lisa's initial twist on Joe's DBQs, assigning the responsibility for constructing questions to the teachers. A manifestation of the doubting Bogart calls out above is there in Joe and Drew's questioning of how colleagues were applying the BBQ, that is, that they had become "too 'facty" and 'worksheety'" rather than serving as an analytical tool. In both cases, and numerous others across the development of the strategy, questions and alternatives were treated as "complementary offers" that extend and heighten the previous turn (Sawyer, 2003), rather than negations of the value of one another's practice or professional knowledge. In other words, they were integrated into the ongoing rhythm of collective creation.

Composition and "Yes, and . . . ," are modes that demand encouragement, modeling, and practice. The next chapter explores the lessons from theatre arts directors about how these key activities can be enacted by coaches, teacher leaders, and others involved in facilitating TLGs. But first, let's take a quick trip back to Cooper Elementary School.

RETURN TO COOPER ELEMENTARY SCHOOL

In the previous chapter, collective creation was examined within individual meetings of a single inquiry group over about a year and a half. The group created resources for the teachers' instruction and their professional learning, in particular, a strategy for incorporating ("test-like") writing prompts, an analytical category for students' writing (personal *and* interesting to the student writer); and what was described as a perspective on teaching as experimentation.

In reviewing these products, it is possible to place them on a continuum of exquisite pressure to cumulative progression. The strategy of "throw some of these [writing prompts] in there" is the most unambiguous manifestation of exquisite pressure. The teachers were, as Bogart and Landau (2005) describe actors doing Composition exercises, "writing on their feet."

The strategy that emerged, however, is limited in its application to the range of purposes for writing that students would encounter. It is not surprising, perhaps, that there is little evidence in later meetings of this strategy being used regularly, even by Devin, its chief author.

The identification of an analytical category for student writing—that is, writing that is not only personal but also reflects a genuine interest of the student—can also be viewed as an outcome of exquisite pressure. In fact, it is the teachers' response to the "score" proposed by Steve Seidel when the steps of the protocol had been finished—that is, identify one compelling question or conundrum that emerged in the prior discussion—that encourages the rapid articulation of the analytical category.

The analytical category, as a conceptual resource, can also be understood as a product of cumulative progression in that it integrated earlier learning experiences of the group. These experiences include the group's earliest discussions, during which they identified questions to investigate. Most of these were related to students' writing development; Lynn's question, in particular, focused on how students can be encouraged to develop independence in their writing—a question the group associated with different kinds of writing tasks students were given.

In first-year meetings, the group examined samples of students' writing in response to a range of assignments (including the common test-like prompt). Over time, based on the evidence of students' actual writing, a hypothesis emerged that assignments that elicited "personal writing" also produced stronger writing. In the meeting that focused on Lynn's student's piece about her personal hero, the group's discovery that writing about something personal was not sufficient, or at least not as effective, in promoting strong writing as writing about something that was also of interest to the student—as Julius Caesar was to one of Lynn's fifth graders.

The analytical category that links these two dimensions of writing is at once a moment of exquisite pressure, a response to the score, and a manifestation of cumulative progression, integrating learning experiences from different points in the group's history.

The third product, an understanding of teaching as experimentation, is identified as performance-as-product because it describes the dynamic of the group's interaction itself, one that is being composed even as it is being enacted. The encouragement for Devin to "sort of experiment with *Rascal*," in particular, in how he relates his own experiences to the characters in the book as a model for students' writing, emerges from the group's examination of his students' reading logs. In this sense, it responds to the pressure of time constraints and a set of steps for the discussion that begins with describing the evidence and formulating questions for the presenting teacher.

Viewed on a longer timescale, however, the episode illustrates how the group's prior investigations of student writing, and in particular, how the teacher introduces and supports students in their writing, are integrated within a product that can be applied within the teachers' classrooms and within the ongoing professional learning of the group. It integrates lessons about how much teacher talk and what kinds of talk best support students' writing, about what kinds of assignments spark students' interests and response, and about the use of student writing samples (and other materials related to them) as evidence in an ongoing process of inquiry.

What is not clear from this episode or others that followed is the group's (including my own) recognition of the nature and value of the performance-as-product they have composed. This is perhaps a reflection of the typical mode of TLGs, in which participants are more attuned to concrete, short-term instructional resources that appear to solve an immediate problem than more abstract and overarching conceptual resources the groups might apply to their ongoing professional learning, as well as their own classrooms.

~

In the episodes from Park East, as well as from Cooper Elementary School, collective creation took place on multiple timescales, in short bursts of exquisite pressure and unfolding over time through cumulative progression. Both can support teacher learning and instructional improvement.

As educators, we have come to rely too heavily on the short-term products and not on creating the conditions that support those products that require ongoing attention and interaction, including inquiry questions, instructional strategies, frameworks and analytical categories for student learning, and others. In short, we do a much better job of generating possibilities—many of which do help to address immediate needs—than composing the kinds of performances that support deep learning over time and meaningful instructional improvement.

The reasons for such an imbalance are multiple and include limited time for teachers to collaborate; demands to carry out prescribed curricula and instruction, often driven by the goal of improving student test scores; absence of leadership or facilitation capacity; teacher turnover; and many others. These are very real problems, but if schools are to become spaces for teachers' learning that foster meaningful and substantive instructional improvement, then educators must develop the tools and orientations to their work to make that learning happen—on both timescales.

The next chapter will consider how collective creation can be realized in TLGs: What are the means necessary to initiate and sustain collective creation, including the use of structures and tools, such as inquiry cycles and discussion protocols, as well as the roles in the process for coaches, facilitators, and lead teachers? How can we expand and deepen our appreciation of the materials that are available for collective creation, including student work, teachers' reflections on their own practice, data on student achievement, curriculum resources, texts of all kinds, and materials the group itself generates through episodes of exquisite pressure? And how do we critically reflect on our modes of engagement so that our activity produces instructional and conceptual resources that support students' learning—and our own?

NOTE

1. With one exception (the pseudonym Caitlin) the names of all teachers and administrators at the Park East Secondary School are their own and are used with permission.

6

Putting Collective Creation to Work

> If you had opened the door of the rehearsal room when we first began, you might have thought you were in a prop maker's workshop, a secondhand clothes store, or even a hallucinatory jam session, with the participants playing desks instead of drums and dancing with coats instead of partners. We used anything which came to hand to find a landmark and open up directions in which to travel. (MacBurney & Complicite, 2003, p. 4)

Simon MacBurney's description of the Complicite company's creation of *The Street of Crocodiles* (based on stories of Bruno Schulz) evokes sites of activity and creativity—a workshop, a clothing store, a musicians' jam session. Alas, he does not include the teachers room among these.

This chapter seeks to redress that gap by using theatre arts ideas and practices to investigate two tightly related dimensions necessary to initiate and sustain teacher learning as collective creation: (1) a process for composition and (2) a role for direction. The first describes how teacher learning groups (TLGs) deliberately structure the means, materials, and modes of engagement of their work to generate learning and instructional improvement. To be effective in doing so, the composition process requires direction, but a form of direction far different from the stereotypical images of the theatre director as artistic genius or dictator (or both).

Rethinking process and direction does not demand rejection of the practices of teacher inquiry groups, critical friends groups, PLCs (professional learning communities), and other vehicles for collaborative learning and instructional improvement. Instead, as becomes clear, TLGs of these and other stripes can enhance their effectiveness by inflecting and infusing their work with ideas and practices of collective creation. Indeed, examples of practices from such groups illustrate how elements of collective creation are already being realized—albeit without referring to them as such.

A PROCESS FOR COMPOSITION

The means for collective creation are not qualitatively different from those already available to schools—and employed by some. Many existing structures and tools support collaborative curriculum planning, teacher inquiry, and other forms of teacher learning. And many of the materials for collective creation are the same ones employed in these forms of teacher learning (for example, samples of student work, teacher-created instructional tools, assessment instruments, assessment data, content-based instructional resources, and others).

What will make a difference for groups is the mode of engagement in which they apply these means and use these materials. That is, whether they view their collaborative activity as the implementation of ready-made curriculum and instruction or as the composition of their own professional learning and instructional change.

The previous chapter explored the idea of collective creation unfolding over time, that is, how groups generate, select, and integrate materials that are identified and developed at different times and in different settings. For example, recall the Ghost Road Company's methods and the development of *Hotel Cassiopeia* by Charles Mee and the SITI Company; in both examples, creating, performing, and discussing Composition pieces is always cumulative, with new pieces integrating selected elements from earlier ones.

Theatre artists encourage this cumulative progression through the use of explicit structures. For example, Bogart and Landau (2005) employ a set of steps for creating compositions. These pieces, in turn, offer possibilities to exploit in developing the script for performance (and the performance itself). The steps begin with identifying "building blocks" for the work, including a question or theme to initiate the process. Subsequent steps include creating, performing, and reflecting on compositions like those described in chapter 3.

Perhaps the most common structures used by TLGs to initiate and guide their work are inquiry cycles. These structures echo Bogart and Landau's method for Composition in intriguing ways. Like it, inquiry cycles generally begin with identifying inquiry questions, then move to collecting artifacts or data from classrooms related to these questions. Like the Composition exercises used by SITI Company, the Ghost Road Company, and other theatre artists, inquiry cycles culminate in the creation of products.

The products of inquiry cycles are typically instructional strategies to apply in participants' classrooms. Some inquiry cycles encourage the creation of other products as well. For example, the Evidence Process ("gears diagram") used by the Cooper Elementary School inquiry group described in chapter 4 locates "identifying and revising inquiry questions" in the center of the cycle, suggesting that inquiry questions are a key product, as well as a driver, of the process.

In the Cycle of Inquiry and Action developed by the Coalition of Essential Schools, pictured in chapter 1 (figure 1.2), the final step is to "Develop [a] vision for teaching and learning" (Cushman, 1999). The Teacher-Research Cycle described by Donald Freeman (1998) even includes the step of "'publishing'—making public," testifying to the value of communicating those products to the larger school community and beyond (see figure 6.1).

In these structures, the creation of products includes but extends beyond discrete instructional resources teachers can apply in their classrooms. Instead, these cycles demonstrate that teacher inquiry processes can result in the creation of conceptual resources—inquiry questions, analytical categories and frameworks for student learning, metaphors, and so on. Like the performances of theatre artists engaged in collective creation, these resources integrate elements of the group's experiences over time.

For TLGs, the goal is to make the learning derived from experience available for the group's ongoing professional learning and application in individual teachers' classrooms. Consider, for example, the strategy for supporting students' analytical writing at Park East High School or the understanding of teaching as experimentation at Cooper Elementary School (see chapter 5).

The process for collective creation for TLGs proposed below builds on structures like these, infused with lessons and tools from the theatre arts. It highlights four essential forms of activity that contribute to the creation of instructional and conceptual resources: (1) framing a question or problem, (2)

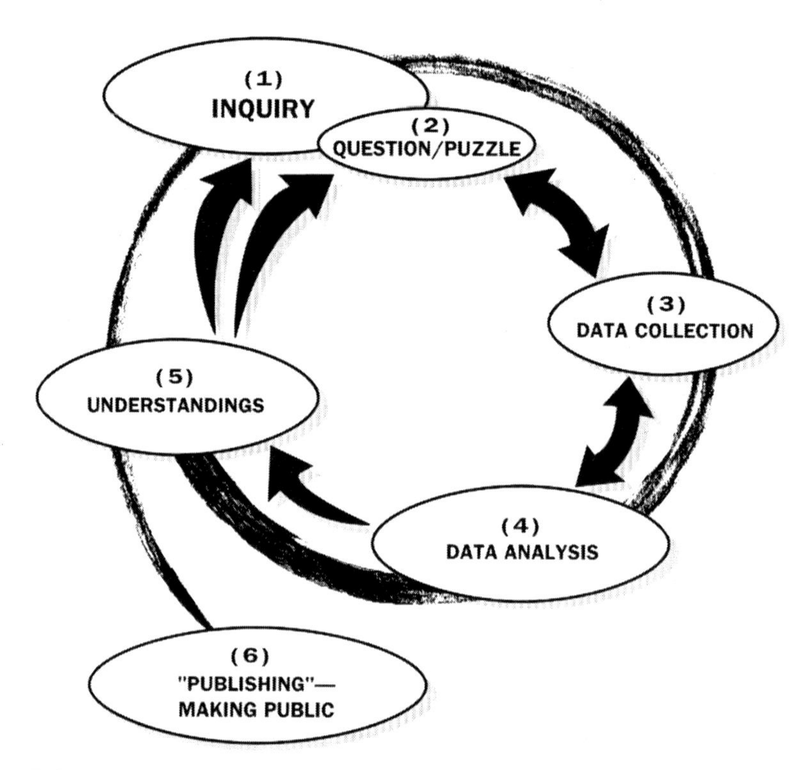

FIGURE 6.1
Cycle of Teacher Research. From Freeman, *Doing Teacher Research* © 1998 Heinle/ELT, a part of Cengage Learning, Inc. Reproduced with permission.

gathering materials, (3) exploring possibilities, and (4) composing resources. The figure below indicates some of the ways each activity might be carried out within TLGs (figure 6.2); many of these will be described in the sections that follow.

Like the structures used by Bogart and Landau, Noon, Halprin, and other theatre artists, this one is not meant to be rigidly linear or prescriptive; rather it should serve as an open, responsive framework for the group's activity. In part because it is so open and flexible, its effectiveness will rely upon attentive and skillful direction, a topic for the second half of the chapter.

Essential Activity	*Sample Action Steps*
Framing the question	➢ Survey participants' interests ➢ Brainstorm possible questions ➢ Play back possible questions
Gathering materials	➢ Identify range of materials available (using "palette of materials") ➢ Generate new materials (e.g. listing, freewriting) ➢ Identify "baby steps" already taken
Exploring possibilities	➢ "Lateral thinking" ➢ "Generate-Sort-Connect-Extend" ➢ Visualize possibilities ➢ Create metaphors
Composing resources	➢ Role-play ➢ Projection ("instructional rehearsal") ➢ Score for composing

FIGURE 6.2
Essential activities and action steps.

Framing the Question

A widespread claim suggests the average classroom teacher will make over fifteen hundred educational decisions every school day. I have yet to find the research that actually supports this claim; for anyone who has taught or observed classrooms, however, it is dramatically if not empirically true. There is no doubt that teachers encounter an enormous number and variety of problems that call for decision making, far more than they can actually devote much time to, individually or in collaboration with colleagues.

Before considering how TLGs decide on which problems to devote their time and energy, it is important to recognize that the activity of deciding itself demands attention and deliberation. This runs counter to a familiar tendency for educators (and others) of reacting to the most immediately apparent problem or the one with the most immediate consequences—colloquially referred to as "putting out fires." To initiate collective creation as cumulative progression requires the group to resist this tendency in order to probe for questions and problems that may be bigger or more obdurate than the day-to-day, moment-to-moment ones that leap out at us.

This is not to suggest TLGs undertake an elaborate formal needs assessment to formulate their focal question or problem, although doing so could be quite useful. Instead, some fairly simple tools, used within a meeting, can help a group frame a problem that is likely to motivate a process that will support meaningful and robust teacher learning and instructional change.

In the Evidence Project at Project Zero, we developed the Finding a Question Protocol for groups to assess potential inquiry questions. A teacher presents his or her "candidate question" and responds to three prompts: (1) Why is this question personally important to you? (2) How is this question relevant to teaching and learning in other classrooms? (3) What direct connections to student learning can we identify? After the presenting teacher speaks, other teachers in the group share their perspectives on the second and third questions.

This is the protocol the group at Cooper Elementary School used to formulate its questions, including the umbrella question about supporting students' writing across the curriculum. In that group and others that used the protocol, candidate questions were almost never rejected; however, they were often clarified or given focus, making them more likely to promote substantive and generative discussions.

The Making Learning Visible (MLV) project, also based at Project Zero, uses a similar protocol with the groups of teachers with which it works. The MLV protocol adds several questions, including: "Is the question aesthetically pleasing to you and others?" Discussing this feature reminds TLGs that their mode of engagement here is not problem-solving or evaluating existing practice but rather composing new resources for their own learning and instructional improvement. It encourages participants in the group to view their work through the eyes of creators.

Another question to add is: "Do we have a clear idea of what the solution or product will look like?" If the answer is yes, then the problem is not open enough for collective creation (though it may well benefit from refinement by the group). If the answer is no (or "hell, no!"), then the group is likely to be operating in a promising mode for collective creation. Figure 6.3 describes a Framing the Question Protocol that integrates ideas from both protocols cited earlier.

Groups might also begin by brainstorming a host of questions or problems, then identifying patterns and prioritizing the ones that generate the most interest and urgency within the group. Sometimes it is useful to involve the perspective of someone with a little distance from the teachers' experi-

1. Why is this question personally important to you?
2. How is it relevant to teaching and learning in other classrooms?
3. What direct connections to student learning can we identify?
4. Is the question aesthetically pleasing to you and others?
5. Do we have a clear idea of what the solution or product will look like? (If no, proceed!)

FIGURE 6.3
Framing the Question Protocol.

ence. For example, a coach or administrator (or researcher) might listen to the discussion and then paraphrase and "play back" what he or she hears: "It sounds to me like the problem has to do with . . ." This is not the same as choosing, but it can help the group to make a choice.

Like other protocols, this one seeks to engender "exquisite pressure," those deliberate constraints (especially on time) that theatre artists find so productive (see chapter 5). Here, the goal is to encourage the group to choose a problem in order to move on to the next steps: gathering materials, exploring possibilities, and so on.

What if the group already has some idea of the shape the product might take, for example, an assessment of students' critical thinking skills, integration of common core standards into project-based curriculum, or a way to encourage peer-to-peer professional exchanges? This can provide an advantage over starting from scratch; however, if the shape of the product is already well-defined, it will limit opportunities for collective creation.

In such a case, the group might begin by probing the assumptions that have led to this projected product: What are the problem(s) it is meant to address? Are there other ways that the problem might be fruitfully addressed? Responding to these questions first will generate materials that expand the scope of possibility for the product that is ultimately composed, even if its broad outlines are established from the outset.

Gathering Materials

One of the chief lessons educators can learn from theatre artists is the wide range of materials available for collective creation. In MacBurney's depiction of the process of the creation for *The Street of Crocodiles*, he reports the company "used anything which came to hand to find a landmark and open up directions in which to travel" (MacBurney & Complicite, 2003, p. 4).

Theatre artists like those in Complicite think expansively about the materials they can identify for collective creation. These include everything from texts to objects, to movement and gestures, to metaphors and images—for instance, the image of a character waiting for a phone call that Bogart offered her actors (see introduction). For TLGs, it is equally important to consider the range of materials available, both the outer materials (those things that one can pick up or point to, such as samples of student work, teacher-created documents, assessment data) and the inner materials groups may tend to overlook (stories, images, metaphors, and more).

An example of how different types of materials were brought together was presented in chapter 4 when the teachers in Cooper Elementary School group presented samples of students' writing on the "unassisted writing prompts," accounts of students at work on the task, students' reflections on their performance, teachers' reports on their own writing instruction, and even their emotional responses to their students' performance.

Another example is found in the creation of the Book-Based Questions (BBQs) at Park East High School, as described in chapter 5. Here, samples of students' writing on the BBQs and stories of how the BBQs were used in different classrooms all proved critical to the composition of a schoolwide strategy for supporting students' analytical writing.

In the Evidence Project, we often talked about how participants in the group could expand the "palette" of evidence they gathered and presented in their meetings. It's a visual arts metaphor rather than a theatrical one, but it works equally well in thinking about collective creation. Figure 6.4 represents how such a palette might be constructed for use by TLGs; it is not intended to be exhaustive, but rather to provide some starting points for groups in thinking about the rich variety of materials they might draw on in their processes.

Theatre artists also recognize the necessity of generating materials more or less on the spot, for example, in the ways Charles Mee and Katharine Noon use lists and free writes to generate materials that respond to a question or problem (see chapter 3). TLGs can also generate materials on the spot. For example, I facilitated an end-of-year reflection of the "Friends with Benefits" group at Park East High School, a voluntary professional development group that meets before first period on some Friday mornings. I asked the teachers to take a few minutes to individually visualize, then write about, one specific moment that stood out for them, for any reason, from any of the group's meetings over the year.

What students create:

- Written pieces (essays, reports, journals, etc.): final or draft
- Visual pieces (essays, reports, journals, etc.)
- Projects
- Performances (e.g., skits, debates, PowerPoint presentations)
- Self-assessments

What students say, do, and think:

- Reflections on their learning and performance (written, oral)
- Comments and questions during classroom discussions
- Visual representations of their thinking/learning (e.g., concept maps)
- Photo/video/audio records of classroom interactions
- Teachers' accounts of classroom interaction (e.g., student discussions during groupwork)

What teachers create:

- Curriculum pieces (e.g., unit plans, lesson plans)
- Assignments
- Tests and quizzes
- Assessment instruments (e.g., rubrics)
- Models (e.g., for student writing, problem-solving, etc.)
- Resources (e.g., checklists, timelines, etc.)

What teachers say, do, and think:

- Reflections on their instruction and student learning (written, oral)
- Comments and questions during TLG meetings (and other forms of professional development)
- Visual representations of their learning (e.g., concept maps)
- Metaphors
- Photo/video/audio records of TLG meetings
- Teachers' accounts of TLG meetings

Other materials:

- Data from standardized tests
- Curriculum resources and teaching aids
- Research (e.g., from journal articles)
- Content-related texts

FIGURE 6.4
Palette for Gathering Materials.

Teachers wrote about instances when the group provided helpful feedback on a specific instructional strategy, for example, using a new rubric for problem solving, but also about moments when the group provided emotional support. For example, one teacher recounted how important it was to meet with colleagues in the group on the morning after he had been involved in breaking up a student altercation. Elements from these stories became materials for defining the benefits and purposes for the group, including providing a site for support, reflection, and feedback on instruction.

Exploring Possibilities

A rich and diverse set of materials can seem like puzzle pieces scattered across a table. In collective creation, there is always more than one way to put the pieces together to construct something new. The tendency for teachers (or actors) eager for a solution may be to focus on the first possibility to emerge and then run with it. This can be beneficial in those very brief meetings that are intended to produce one clear solution to an immediate problem, as illustrated in chapter 5 in the teachers' meetings with the coach. However, as noted there, doing so often precludes the potential for composing resources that are more powerful and enduring in supporting teacher learning and instructional change.

In progressing from raw materials to composed resources, TLGs spend significant time with the materials: appreciating the individual qualities of each; asking how they may relate to one another; and allowing multiple possibilities that address the question to emerge. Bogart and Landau adopt de Bono's (1990) concept of "lateral thinking," or exploring relationships among materials, recognizing its potential to generate new possibilities and thus new materials for the ongoing composition of a piece.

This is very close to Dewey's (1910) definition of reflective thinking as the perception of relationships among different aspects of experience. Lateral thinking is a mode of engagement that asks teachers to restrain, at least for a little while, the familiar tendency to make a quick decision. Instead, it demands we attend closely to the materials at hand and be open to discovering relationships among them.

A useful tool to support lateral thinking is Generate-Sort-Connect-Elaborate (see figure 6.5), one of many classroom strategies known as "thinking routines" (Ritchhart, Church, & Morrison, 2011). This strategy asks participants not only to identify possible relationships among ideas, but also to explain or speculate on the nature of the connections, which in turn generates new materials/possibilities for the composition of instructional or conceptual resources.

Select a topic, concept, or issue for which you want to map your understanding.

Generate a list of ideas and initial thoughts that come to mind when you think about this particular topic/issue.

Sort your ideas according to how central or tangential they are. Place central ideas near the center and more tangential ideas toward the outside of the page.

Connect your ideas by drawing connecting lines between ideas that have something in common. Explain and write in a short sentence how the ideas are connected.

Elaborate on any of the ideas/thoughts you have written so far by adding new ideas that expand, extend, or add to your initial ideas.

Continue generating, connecting, and elaborating new ideas until you feel you have a good representation of your understanding.

FIGURE 6.5
Generate-Sort-Connect-Elaborate. From Ritchhart, Church, & Morrison, *Making Thinking Visible* © 2011 Jossey Bass. Used with permission.

While Generate-Sort-Connect-Elaborate is a tool for generating ideas and initial thoughts, it can be used just as beneficially with materials already on the table (for example, samples of student work, teachers' observations of students at work, assessment data, curriculum standards, texts, images, etc.). In this case, the generation of new materials simply responds to prior steps of examining the existing materials and identifying possible relationships among them—a step often slighted in an eagerness to get on with solving the problem.

Not all versions of exploring possibilities follow a strict protocol or routine. For example, my colleague Tina Blythe and I work with a group of lead teachers from schools in Santiago, Chile. Each has been facilitating a small group of teachers in his or her own school. The groups were formed to support teachers in studying and applying the Teaching for Understanding framework for developing curriculum and assessments (Blythe & Associates, 1998).

In the second year of their work, a second cohort of teachers was formed at each of the schools, while the original groups continued to meet. One of the problems the lead teachers identified was how to assist the newly formed cohort in each school when it was not possible for the lead teacher to attend most of the new cohort's meetings. We asked the teacher leaders to brainstorm multiple possibilities for working with both groups at their school. We also asked them to note any promising initial actions ("baby steps") they had already taken to address the problem.

As the group looked for connections among the ideas and accounts that emerged, we began to visualize a "dynamic" (in the words of one of the teachers) that might exist between the two cohorts within each school. This metaphor itself became material for the composition of professional development strategies for the schools, which included joint meetings of the groups, presentations by a cohort 1 teacher in cohort 2, peer observations and feedback, and others.

Composing Resources

For theatre artists, Composition exercises, like those described in chapter 3, force participants to "write on their feet" (Bogart & Landau, 2005). This strategy moves actors away from talking about what they might do and to begin doing it, that is, composing performances. As Katharine Noon told my Composition group, the sooner you get on your feet and start trying out ideas, the more successful your composition will be—and, believe me, my group needed to hear that!

Teachers in TLGs may experience a similar, if not stronger, reluctance to leave the relative safety of talking through problems and possible solutions—after all, isn't that how we solve problems? In fact, examples are at hand of teachers embracing more active, embodied approaches to instructional improvement and professional learning. Consider, for example, the two student teachers in chapter 2 who physically try out ways to illustrate for students the concept of adding rates of motion (Hall, 1996), and the groups of novice bilingual teachers who act out professional conflicts they have experienced and ways to address them (Cahnmann-Taylor, Wooten, and Souto-Manning & Dice, 2009).

These examples provide images of the power of performing as a way of thinking with the theatre arts. Another approach is to collectively imagine, or project, how an instructional strategy might play out within the classroom context, what Horn (2010) refers to as "instructional rehearsals." These strategies can be embedded in a deliberate process for composing resources. The framework—or score, to use the language of the RSVP Cycles (chapter 3)—for such a process is outlined in figure 6.6.

Like the protocol for framing a question or the Generate-Sort-Connect-Elaborate thinking routine, this score is intended to exploit the power of exquisite pressure. It is designed to be "doable" in one meeting. Of course, the group can decide how much pressure to apply here, but in general, the first four activity steps (naming through performing) should be brief (roughly five to ten minutes each) and feel dynamic, even frenetic; the last two steps, reflection and recording, might take more time but without losing the sense of forward movement.

Supporting a single episode of exquisite pressure, especially if it generates instructional resources teachers can use, has value in its own right. To use the tools of exquisite pressure, like those identified above, to sustain a more extended process of cumulative progression and achieve more robust instructional and conceptual resources, requires direction, a role considered in the next section.

Name the target: The specific question or problem being addressed (e.g., learning goal, Common Core standard, instructional or professional challenge, etc.)

Specify the "ingredients" to work with: What are the specific materials that must be addressed, in some way, in the work (for example, a learning goal or objective, text, instructional strategy, etc.)?

Compose: Collectively (in pairs or small groups) create *possible* responses that address the target and incorporate the ingredients. Make them as specific as possible, i.e., differentiate actions, use of language, incorporation of texts or other resources, etc.

Perform: Present/represent the compositions (responses) for colleagues—the more actively the better (act it out, map it out, draw it out . . .). The point is to make them available as objects for critical reflection by the group.

Reflect: After a composition has been performed, point to elements (moments, ideas, insights, images, text, etc.) that might be used in a future composition.

Record. Make a record of some kind (in writing, photography, video) of the identified elements. This record might be used right away in a new round of composing or in future meetings.

FIGURE 6.6
Score for Composing Resources.

A ROLE FOR DIRECTION

Advocates for teacher learning as inquiry or professional community may bristle at the use of the word "direction" in relation to the work of TLGs. It smacks of top-down control rather than democratic collaboration. It may even suggest a "contrived collegiality" in which TLGs are pushed to pursue administrative goals at the cost of their own autonomy and agency (Hargreaves & Dawe, 1990; Hargreaves & Fullan, 2012). And they'd be wise to be wary, given the disempowered history of the profession (Lagemann, 2000).

Even stronger associations with the word "direction" haunt theatre arts, in which exists a long tradition of the director as "captain" or "benevolent dictator" (Knowles, 2004). From the start, then, it is vital to separate this familiar but far-from-universal image of "director" from "direction," as embodied by theatre artists like Anne Bogart, Katharine Noon, Anna Halprin, Simon MacBurney, and many other practitioners of collective creation. With these artists' methods, direction seeks to promote within the company the open and participatory composition of works for performance.

Bogart (2001) puts it this way: "It is not the director's responsibility to produce results but, rather, to create the circumstances in which something might happen" (p. 124). How directors create these conditions offers important lessons for TLGs engaged in collective creation.

If direction is understood as a role rather than a person, it becomes possible to identify particular dispositions and skills that contribute to its effectiveness. In working with nonactors, the director and educator Augusto Boal (1979) was challenged with encouraging participants to engage in his methods for exploring and confronting oppression: Theatre of the Oppressed, Forum Theatre, and others. To do so, he created a "Joker" figure whose task is to "facilitate but not control the theatre event" (Babbage, 2004, p. 143).

The Joker establishes the guidelines for the activity, invites participants into the activity, assists, and provides summaries of emerging solutions to the problem being explored. Lib Spry (1994), who uses Boal's methods as a director, producer, and teacher, writes: "The Joker's job is that of midwife to the process. . . . The Joker must continually find the balance between honoring the process of the group and the needs of an effective final product" (p. 179). This same dual emphasis on inclusive process and meaningful product is precisely what is required for collective creation within TLGs, and there too it requires someone to encourage it.

Directors are not the only ones who can provide direction: "You get two directors on stage and then the actor tells you what to do," Anne Bogart joked during a "talkback" with the audience after a 2008 production of Beckett's *Happy Days* with actress Fiona Shaw and the play's director, Deborah Warner. In theatre arts companies, especially those engaged in collective creation, it is common for members to switch roles for a time: for instance, in the Ghost Road Company actors routinely play each other's parts and often "instigate" a process of free writing and Composition exercises like those described in chapter 3 (Noon, 2011). Of course, many actors are also full-fledged directors in their own right.

While more than one participant in a TLG might play the role of director at different points, for a group's work to succeed, someone *must* play it. This person might be a lead teacher, a facilitator, a coach, or even an administrator—provided he or she is committed to a process of composition, has and develops the skills to support the group's collective creation (more to come about this), and has time and energy to devote to the role. These requirements are similar to the kinds of facilitation specified by other forms of teacher learning, including teacher inquiry, teacher research, and professional learning communities (Allen & Blythe, 2004; McLaughlin & Talbert, 2006).

The sections that follow treat three dimensions of direction necessary for collective creation in TLGs, especially for the longer-term cumulative progression that results in potent resources for instructional change and deep teacher learning: (1) creating conditions for collective creation, (2) sustaining the process, (3) reflecting on process and celebrating accomplishment. Here, the reader will find fewer of the tools that populated the first half of the chapter: direction is a way of thinking about how to use these tools to be productive.

Creating Conditions

In creating conditions for collective creation, theatre directors identify a question, problem, or theme that will be of genuine interest to their collaborators. They also introduce a structure that will support the company's exploration of the question and foster composition of a piece for performance. Facilitators or coaches committed to teacher learning as collective creation within TLGs undertake similar actions with different problems and products in view.

As described earlier in the chapter, collective creation, in the black box theatre or the teachers' room, typically responds to a problem or question—but not to any old problem or question. There must be a genuine interest in a given problem or question among participants for it to drive a process of composition. Thus, an important responsibility of direction is to sound the group for questions or problems related to instruction and student learning that are of interest and import to all participants. This might be done formally or informally, through free writing exercises, questionnaires, or discussion; for collective creation to occur, however, someone must deliberately make the question or problem explicit as a focus for the group's collective activity.

In the Evidence Project and Making Learning Visible methods, external facilitators and teacher facilitators from the groups used protocols, like the one in figure 6.3, as tools for discovering the questions of interest to participants in the group. In Suzy Ort's coaching at Park East High School (see chapter 5), she often employed a less formal approach: talking to teachers individually and in group meetings, then playing back for teachers the questions or problems she discerned as interesting to the teachers and important for the school. Tina Blythe and I used a similarly dialogic approach with the lead teachers in Santiago. However it is undertaken, the goal is for the group to "own" a question it will be eager to address.

A fundamental activity of direction, which extends the discovery of interest and identification of a question or problem to work on, is to find a structure for collective creation. As Peter Brook (1968) observes, "Any rehearsal technique has its use, . . . no technique is all-embracing" (p. 124). Theatre artists are continually adopting, adapting, and adjusting structures and tools that will work for the question at hand and for the group with whom they are working.

Similarly, in TLGs, there is no single structure that will work in every setting to effectively support the composition of instructional and conceptual resources. Some of the structures that have been effective are described earlier in this chapter, in particular, the inquiry cycles developed by the Coalition of Essential Schools, the Evidence Project, and other projects. Exactly how such structures are used to promote collective creation are determined by the culture and organization of the school, the nature of the group's question or problem, and the individual teachers involved.

At Park East High School, by contrast, there was no preexisting structure in place for the composition of the BBQ strategy for supporting students' textual analysis and writing. Instead, collective creation occurred through the coordination, largely by the coach, of existing configurations of teachers and uses of professional time: individual and group meetings of teachers, a teacher-led professional development committee and the whole-faculty professional development sessions the committee planned, as well as regular meetings of the coach and school administrators. Suzy also seized on informal opportunities to advance collective creation, for example, hallway encounters and email or phone conversations with teachers and administrators.

This kind of direction calls for a sense of timing that mirrors that of theatre directors. Brook (1968) writes, "A director has to have a sense of time: it is for him to feel the rhythm of the process and observe its divisions" (p. 125). In similar fashion, a coach, teacher leader, or facilitator of a TLG will make judgments about when the time is right for a particular activity, for instance, using Generate-Sort-Connect-Elaborate as a means for exploring possibilities generated in a meeting.

There are many resources for facilitators of inquiry groups and PLCs, just as there are for theatre artists engaged in collective creation or devised theatre. Some of these outline full-fledged inquiry processes (Evidence Project Staff, 2001; Freeman, 1998; Shagoury & Power, 2012); others provide discussion protocols and other tools that can be employed within different processes (Easton, 2009; McDonald, Mohr, Dichter, & McDonald, 2007). (The appendix provides references for these resources.)

Even with a plethora of tools available, direction sometimes demands invention, that is, adapting an existing tool or creating a new one in response to the group's activity. More challenging still, this demand for invention often occurs in the moment of activity itself, leaving the facilitator little time for reflection and planning. In such moments, the director or facilitator proposes a new (or adapted) score for the group to use, as Anna Halprin did with the nondancers in *Dancing with Life on the Line* (see chapter 3) or as Tina Blythe and I did by asking the lead teachers in Santiago to recall "baby steps" they had tried with the teacher groups they facilitate.

Like other responsibilities of direction, invention of scores takes practice and benefits from critical self-reflection by the facilitator and his or her group. Making opportunities to discuss facilitation scenarios, moves, and dilemmas with other facilitators is also a very useful way to develop judgment and skills for in-the-moment decision making.

Whether or not there is an explicit structure from the beginning or a tried-and-true set of tools, direction helps the group address key procedural questions: what will we do when we come together? (an exquisite pressure question) and how will the activity in one meeting build on or extend the experiences in the ones that came before? (a cumulative progression question). Of course, a facilitator or coach does not—and should not—determine the answer to these questions. Instead, direction involves constantly communicating the group's collective responsibility for identifying a question or problem, gathering materials, exploring possibilities, and ultimately composing resources that address the problem.

Sustaining the Process

For a theatre arts company, the necessity of sustaining a process of collective creation is self-evident: the existence and quality of the piece it will ultimately perform depends on it. In schools, in which teachers are called upon to perform a myriad of tasks every day—lesson planning, providing instruction, grading, communicating with students' families, to name just a few—the need for sustenance is even greater. And in schools, depending on a group's meeting schedule, the process is likely to be interrupted by days or weeks at a time, making attention to sustaining it all the more critical.

Many activities that administrators, lead teachers, facilitators, or coaches undertake to sustain collective creation reflect the activities of theatre directors. Here three categories of action are highlighted, each with strong overlap with the tools for cumulative progression described in chapter 5: attention, recording, and selection.

Attention

Anne Bogart (2001) identifies attention as "the only real gift I can offer to an actor" (p. 74). It is that and more: the director's attention to all aspects of the creation process—from the earliest discussions about a question to explore, to the dress and technical rehearsals that precede opening night—provides the platform for all of the other actions that sustain the process of cumulative progression.

This kind of heightened attention was evident in Suzy Ort's coaching at Park East. For example, she paid close attention to what was going on in

Drew and Lisa's classroom as they experimented with the early versions of the BBQs. Later, she picked up on Drew and Joe's dissatisfaction with how some other teachers were applying the strategy, which led to a full-faculty professional development session about using BBQs. Both moments might have passed unheeded but for the quality of the coach's attentive eye for possibilities (materials) for collective creation.

Attention can also be appreciated in its absence. In the Cooper Elementary School inquiry group meeting where the strategy of incorporating ("throwing in") unassisted writing prompts was created, neither Nora, the teacher facilitator, nor I caught—or at least called the group's attention to—a provocative question. That was the moment when Toni asked Devin whether his way of teaching writing was the right way (implying the state's way of assessing it might be the wrong one).

To have highlighted this moment, as a facilitator, would have been to disrupt the momentum toward the strategy but it might have led to a richer exploration of the materials teachers had brought to the meeting, and, eventually, to the composition of more robust instructional and conceptual resources.

Recording

The facilitator or coach, any more than a theatre director, cannot be expected to attend to everything that is going on in a given episode. For this reason, if for no other, recording takes on a critical importance to collective creation. For theatre artists, the primary records of the process are the director's and the dramaturge's notes, but they might also include photos and videotapes and other artifacts of Composition exercises and rehearsals.

The Park East coach's notebook, bulging with samples of teachers' assignments, samples of student work, agendas from meetings, and much more, provides a ready image for recording the work of TLGs. The role of direction here is not necessarily to record everything but to support the group in developing and using its own routines for recording its process and products.

In the Evidence Project, group meetings were taped and transcribed by the Evidence Project staff; however, this is time consuming and unlikely to become a regular practice within schools. More practical strategies include designating a note-taker for specific meetings, collecting artifacts from the meetings (agendas, work samples, etc.), and, wherever possible, creating a visual record of the meeting, for instance, photographing any products created during the meeting (e.g., poster, chart, notes on chart paper, etc.). Even these relatively simple kinds of recording rely upon direction: someone coordinates the recording and ensures the record is safe and accessible.

The Making Learning Visible Project has developed tools for documenting students' learning, including a protocol for reflecting on how teachers are documenting students' learning (figure 6.7). Direction in TLGs, thus, continually focuses the group on the question of how it will record its activity and, periodically, how the group uses the record to inform and infuse its process of collective creation.

- Am I documenting my own words and actions as well as the students'?
- Does the documentation help me re-examine things I did not initially notice or understand?
- Does the documentation help me identify key moments of learning or aspects of the learning context?
- Does the documentation suggest next steps for teaching or learning?
- Does the documentation raise questions I can discuss with my colleagues or students?
- What other documentation might I collect to extend this inquiry? Would my documentation be strengthened by using more than one medium?

FIGURE 6.7
Protocol for Documenting Teachers' Reflections. Making Learning Visible Project, Project Zero, Harvard Graduate School of Education. Used with permission.

Selecting

In the introduction, I described a move I have seen Anne Bogart make with actors a number of times. "Do something stupid," she tells performers when something is not working or when they feel stuck. Of course, she does not mean this literally; instead, she is signaling strongly that the actors must make a choice and go with it. In the Open Canvas exercise used by the Pig Iron Company, Quinn Bauriedel called out, for example, "Everybody off except the two dancers." And this selection affected the dynamic of the developing composition as the other performers responded to the dancers.

Katharine Noon in the Ghost Road Company workshop was emphatic that our Composition group choose an image from the dozens of photos available and get to work with it (see chapter 3). The selection a group makes might not work but unless a selection is made from myriad possibilities, movement toward collective creation will sputter.

TLGs often experience a similar paralysis in the face of multiple possibilities. There are so many things to discuss, work on, read, and so forth that groups often wind up not discussing, working on, or reading much of anything—or at least that's the way many meetings feel. Suzy Ort, as coach, employs a mechanism similar to Bogart's when she reminds teachers in a planning discussion at Park East that the idea they go with needs to be "good enough."

By doing so, she is not trying to encourage subpar teaching—or subpar thinking about teaching—but to nudge teachers to select and move forward rather than abandoning a promising possibility for development. What was good enough when applied in one classroom often contributes over time to the composition of effective and robust instructional strategies, like the use of BBQs and other tools for scaffolding students' development of analytical skills.

In the Evidence Project, teachers confessed that, realizing the group's meeting was minutes away, at times they "grabbed" something close at hand to present as evidence, for example, samples of recently completed student work or a rubric they had been using to assess student work. In fact, these discussions were often substantive in relation to the presenting teacher's question. Rather than deny the reality of teachers' overstuffed school days, we made a virtue of the reality, talking about ways to "grab better," in other words, to select quickly but more generatively.

Another example of selection from the project was portrayed in chapter 4. Steve Seidel's proposal that the Cooper inquiry group "come to a pretty carefully articulated statement" of an important question or "conundrum" that emerged in the earlier protocol-guided discussion. This move prompted the group to identify specific qualities of student writing that appeared to lead to stronger writing: that it is personal *and* that the student has a genuine interest in what he or she is writing about.

This analytical category for writing became a resource for the group as it continued to develop its understanding of how to support student writing in an environment increasingly defined by high-stakes testing. It also served as a useful resource for individual teachers in creating writing tasks for their students.

The task for the person providing direction in TLGs here is not to select for the group, but to create the conditions and expectation for the group's selection—often through judicious use of exquisite pressure—as modeled by Suzy and Steve in the examples above. Balancing the need for both more exploration of materials and emerging possibilities than teachers may be accustomed to and the necessity of making a selection from these possibilities, which teachers may resist, is one of the enduring challenges of facilitation or direction.

Reflect and Celebrate

The importance of reflective practice in teaching—or any profession—is well established (Fendler, 2003; Rodgers, 2002; Zeichner & Liston, 1996). However, in encouraging teachers to reflect on their practices, we are often opaque about what actually constitutes reflection. In the theatre arts, it is axiomatic that reflection serves the ongoing creation of a piece; through critically and selectively reviewing prior experience, theatre artists formulate future action.

For theatre artists, the process of reflection is the process of analyzing and choosing which of many possible actions will be the most valuable in moving forward. Valuaction, a component of the RSVP Cycles, links the terms "value" and "action," signaling these fundamentally generative purposes for critical self-reflection (Halprin & Kaplan, 1995).

Valuaction questions that are used to reflect on the performances of a piece (at any stage of the creation process) include: "What worked well?" "What would you like to develop further?" "What new resources (e.g., themes, movement activities, or qualities) have arisen from the score?" "Is the score clear?" "Does it need to be more open or more closed?" "And where do you go from here?" (Worth & Poyner, 2004, pp. 178–79). It is not hard to see the potential value of the same or similar questions for a TLG reflecting on the process and products of its meetings.

The choreographer Liz Lerman has developed a Process for Critical Response to performance that includes separate steps for: (1) statements of meaning, (2) artist as questioner, (3) neutral questions from responders to the performer, and (4) permissioned opinions from responders (Lerman & Borstel, 2003). There is a double purpose here: facilitating the specific kinds of feedback that will contribute to the development of the piece and doing so in a way that is safe and productive for the creator(s) and those offering feedback.

For teacher learning as collective creation, the role for direction is to encourage similarly generative reflection activities. Coaches and facilitators do this in many ways, for example, incorporating reflection as a step within discussion protocols, like those described in chapter 4. Or, at the end of a meeting, the facilitator might ask participants in a group to reflect in writing on questions such as: What's one thing you are going to take away from the meeting? What's one unanswered question? Periodically, the group might devote a meeting or substantial part of a meeting to reflection on the group's process, as the Friends with Benefits group at Park East did. All of these methods support discussions that, when recorded, provide the group materials for its ongoing collective creation process.

Daniel Wilson, another colleague from Project Zero, has developed a tool that differentiates types of feedback and provides a sequence for offering these in relation to a plan or an idea (Wilson, Perkins, Bonnet, Miani, & Unger, 2005). The Ladder of Feedback describes four steps for a group to structure its feedback: (1) clarify, (2) value, (3) state concerns, and (4) suggest (see figure 6.8). The tool can be used by TLGs to reflect on a specific resource composed by the group or on the group's process of collective creation itself.

The steps of the ladder, like Lerman's process above, recognize that teachers, like theatre artists, feel vulnerable and even protective when their work is the object of feedback. As a director participating in a SITI Company intensive workshop told me, sometimes you have to "give the note more space." In other words, find the context that will allow it to be heard by the performer receiving it. Facilitators of TLGs similarly consider how to create conditions in which feedback will be actionable.

Strongly related to critical reflection is the celebration of a group's process and products. At Cambridge Rindge and Latin School, in Massachusetts, a group of teachers working with the Making Learning Visible Project organizes an annual exhibition of teacher learning. Participants in the group create posters that document and tell the story of their learning over the course of the year. They display these in the school's teacher resource center and use them in panel discussions for other teachers from the school. In this way, they not only celebrate their learning but also make it available as resources for other teachers in the school. (Appendix I provides references to the MLV website for more information.)

The idea or plan is presented to the group. Then the group moves through the following steps (moving from one rung of the ladder to the next):

Step 1: Clarify
Ask clarifying questions to be sure you understand the idea or matter on the table. Avoid clarifying questions that are thinly disguised criticism.

Step 2: Value
Express what you like about the idea or matter at hand in specific terms. Do not offer perfunctory "good, but," and hurry on to the negatives.

Step 3: State concerns
State your puzzles and concerns. Avoid absolutes: "What's wrong is . . ." Use qualified terms: "I wonder if . . ." "It seems to me . . ." Avoid criticizing personal character or ability and focus on ideas, products, or particular aspects.

Step 4: Suggest
Make suggestions about how to improve things. This step is sometimes blended with step 3: people state concerns and then offer suggestions for addressing them.

There is no set time limit for this process: It can be done in a few minutes or over the course of an hour.

FIGURE 6.8
Ladder of Feedback. Wilson, Perkins, Bonnet, Miani, & Unger, *Learning at Work* © 2005 President and Fellows, of Harvard College. Used with permission.

More commonly, celebration occurs in less elaborate fashion, often within a TLG group's regular meeting time. Wherever and however it takes place, celebration recognizes that collective creation is demanding as well as rewarding. To create new resources requires more work than to replicate and implement existing ones. In collective creation, teachers often expose aspects of their practices and beliefs that they do not typically allow others to see, breaking the professional norm of isolation. For direction, this does not mean heaping empty praise on participants or on the products of their work; instead, it means creating occasions—one-on-one, within the group, and within the school—to highlight the instructional and conceptual resources the group has produced and its methods for doing so.

Celebration as a responsibility of the role reminds us that direction is no more a technical skill than it is a dictatorial approach. Peter Brook told an interviewer: "I have a very set formula, which is to prevent anything from being set. That is a formula as well" (Croyden, 2003, p. 21). Structures and tools, such as inquiry cycles and protocols, are critical. The skilled facilitator of a TLG recognizes, along with Brook, Bogart, Noon, Lerman, and other directors and choreographers, that allowing a group's activity to become too set is antithetical to creation.

Direction for them is as much about being responsive as it is about being creative. It is about being present with and for the actors with whom you collaborate and trusting that the process you make together can generate worthwhile performances. Why not believe that educators committed to fostering one another's learning and instructional improvement are capable of a similarly engaged presence and trust?

~

Collective creation in TLGs requires commitment to a process that gives deliberate and sustained attention to framing a question or a problem to investigate; gathering and generating materials of many kinds that relate to the problem or question; exploring possibilities that emerge from engaging with the materials; and composing instructional and conceptual resources to apply in the classroom and within the group's ongoing learning. This chapter has provided tools and examples from groups undertaking just these activities; the appendix provides references to more such resources.

Collective creation also requires facilitation as a form of direction that embodies a heightened attention to the interests and activities of the group's participants; skillful use of structures and tools; the capacity to create scores in the moment that foster exquisite pressure; and the judicious exercise of recording, selection, reflection, and celebration to sustain cumulative progression.

The final chapter will highlight some places to begin a journey into collective creation.

7

From Community to Company

Three Cues for Teacher Learning Groups

> A company of actors—in relation to the work that they are performing—is a community. (Chaikin, 1991, p. 28)

The image of the school as a community has been with us at least since Dewey (1900) described the school as a "miniature community, an embryonic society" (p. 32) for children. It is inscribed in the mission statements and names of schools across the country, including the first school I taught in.

The image of teachers within a school as its own community is a much more recent phenomenon, gaining currency only in the last two decades of the twentieth century. By the early years of twenty-first century, the model of professional learning community (PLC) had become a widespread strategy for professional development and instructional improvement, one that highlights collaboration, reflection, and collective responsibility for student learning (Hord, 1997; Grossman, Wineburg, & Woolworth, 2001; Louis, Kruse, & Marks, 1996; Stevens & Kahne, 2006). Teachers, schools, and districts have embraced it.

So it came as something of a surprise, especially in a symposium titled "Teacher Communities in Secondary Education: How Teachers Work and Learn Together," to hear Judith Warren Little ask, "Should we be using the image of community at all?" (AERA, 2011). It was a provocative question, especially in a room full of education researchers and practitioners, many of whom, like me, had studied, participated in, and advocated for teacher learning communities as vehicles for teachers' professional development and instructional improvement. Little proposed as an alternative image the cross-functional team, a model for improving product development and performance in industry, health care, and social services (McDonough, 2003; Randel & Jaussi, 2003). Her comments left unexplored what was wrong with or missing from community as an image for teacher learning—or even what's right about it.

The idea of school as a professional learning community has served to refocus teachers and administrators on the learning that can happen right there in their own school and with their own colleagues. It has validated reflective dialogue and inquiry as legitimate forms of professional development (PD)—opposing these to the one-way transmission of information that had so often counted as PD. And it has underscored teachers' responsibility for their colleagues' learning as well as for their own, eschewing the familiar attitude of every teacher for him- or herself within the sanctuary of his or her classroom. It has also affirmed the professional status of teachers' interactions with colleagues, seeking to reverse a legacy view of teaching as the acquisition and exercise of narrowly defined technical skills rather than the development and deployment of professional knowledge and judgment (Lagemann, 2000).

For many, if not most, teachers participating in groups closely aligned with the goals of professional learning communities, such as inquiry groups, critical friends groups, or those simply referred to as PLCs, the main benefit often boils down the support they receive from and provide for one another. J. C., one of the teachers in the Friends with Benefits group at Park East High School (see chapter 6), paraphrased a colleague in the group:

> I think Darren said it best when he said that all he needed to do was be around teachers, smile, have some bagels, and feel supported. Whether that's in the work that we all create, whether we're throwing ideas at each other, whether we're spending six hours on a Saturday working on something, it's always around the work; it's always evolved around the work.

Feeling supported expands to include the collegial or moral support for dealing with the myriad pressures, stresses, and even conflicts—with colleagues, administrators, the district or system—that teaching entails.

Implicit in J. C.'s comments is the recognition that effective collaboration with colleagues requires a high degree of trust. Increasingly, trusting relationships with colleagues are recognized as a core condition for the effective functioning of learning communities (Bryk & Schneider, 2002; Crowther, 2011). Trusting relationships provide the social capital for instructional and organizational change. They are both a condition for effective TLG practices that focus on teacher learning and student learning—like those portrayed in this book—*and* are strengthened through teachers' participation in those same practices (Hargreaves & Fullan, 2012).

The formulation of PLC has been less helpful in expanding our understanding of the outcomes for the groups' activity, that is, articulating what the inquiry, reflection, support, and trust add up to, beyond a generalized notion of professional learning. It begs the question, in other words, what it is the groups produce. This is partly understandable, given the critical role of school context in determining a TLG's focus, as well as the group's autonomy in defining its goals: no single product will lead professional learning or instructional improvement in every school.

The danger of underspecifying the outcomes or products of a group's activity is that it allows others to define them for the groups, especially those who would limit teachers' professional interactions to "data-based decision-making," where data is synonymous with the results of standardized tests (Hargreaves & Fullan, 2012). Steve Seidel, in his foreword, rightly called out the "educational-industrial complex" of corporate test publishers, professional development providers, and others as ready to supply "teacher-proof" curriculum and assessment materials—no need for collective creation with these!

More positively, this absence of specificity about the products of TLGs' activity invites learning from other domains, particularly from those in which collaboration is inherently and dynamically tied to productivity. Doubtless, we could learn from industrial models like the cross-functional teams Little suggested in her talk. This book has been an inquiry instead into the domain of theatre arts, in which performance *is* the product. Theatre artists' performances-as-products are not only meant to be satisfying, sometimes even enthralling, to their audiences and gratifying to their creators, but they embody the learning experiences of the companies that create them. Substitute "students" for "audiences," and shouldn't the products of TLGs do the same?

This final chapter offers three "cues" for action for educators in or working with teacher learning groups (TLGs): begin with listening, give attention, and emphasize rigorous creation. Whether or not educators choose to see their work in schools as related to that of theatre companies in black box theatres or rehearsal spaces, these cues offer starting places to reevaluate and reconstruct practice within TLGs as vehicles for professional learning community.

BEGIN WITH LISTENING

In a workshop on devised theatre, Quinn Bauriedel of the Pig Iron Theatre Company taught participants a Ukrainian folk song. We stood in a circle about him and practiced the song in parts. Once we had learned the words of the song (though not their meaning), he asked us to close the circle and sing it once again, more slowly and quietly. He asked us to imagine that we were singing it to an imaginary spot about shoulder high in the center of the circle. "It's as much about listening as singing," Quinn told us. In doing so, we reversed a dynamic common to actors or teachers, the impulse to be heard first and listen second.

In the introduction of this book, I assured readers that I would not propose that they take up the theatre games or exercises regularly used by actors, such as the classic "mirror game" used by scene partners or the one used by Fiona Shaw, in which student actors imitate an animal, then speak a Shakespeare soliloquy as that animal (see chapter 3 and appendix). If, however, I were to propose one game or exercise, it would be this simple one I participated in as part of the Ghost Road Company workshop (and have subsequently used with my own students):

- Participants stand in a tight circle, with shoulder blades just touching, *eyes closed.*
- The goal is to count to thirty.
- Any participant can add the next number to the count—but can add only one before another participant speaks.
- If two or more participants speak at the same time, the count must begin again at one.

What at first seemed impossible—for the sixteen of us to reach thirty without anyone talking over anyone else—became easier in the course of just a few minutes. What changed? We learned to listen to each other, to the rhythms of the group, to the words (numbers) spoken, and to the silences.

Anne Bogart (2001) reminds us, "Rehearsal is not about forcing things to happen; rather it is about listening. The director listens to the actors. The actors listen to one another. You listen collectively to the text. You listen for clues. You keep things moving. You probe" (p. 125). Far from a passive receiving, listening becomes active inquiry, a reaching out for materials that may contribute to the group's collective creation.

Peter Brook puts it succinctly, "Listening is more important than doing . . . doing is the result of good listening. Which is what I drum into our actors all the time" (Croyden, 2003, pp. 274–75). In other words, the quality of what we do (ask, respond, compose, reflect, etc.) depends on the quality with which we listen. For Brook, Bogart, Noon, Bauriedel, and other theatre artists, it is axiomatic that listening can be learned.

Begin with listening because listening is fundamental to communication within a company or community. The quality of that communication will enable other forms of collective attention. Like actors engaged in collective creation, teachers in TLGs ask questions, offer suggestions, and provide feedback on our performances. The quality with which we do all these depends on the quality with which we listen to one another.

A simple but powerful tool educators have developed to highlight and practice listening is the Micro Lab Protocol, in which groups of three are asked to respond to an open-ended question. After a period of silent reflection and writing, each participant in a group has a minute (or 90 seconds) to respond—without interruption, questioning, "I know what you mean . . . ," etc. (see Ritchhart, Church, & Morrison, 2011, p. 147). When I have used this protocol, teachers often report how difficult it is not to interrupt their colleagues when they are speaking and how rare it is to be listened to for even a minute.

The cue for action for educators is to critically reflect on the quality of our listening within TLGs and develop means to practice it. To do so, we might use practices like the Micro Lab Protocol or adopt some of the practices of theatre artists.

GIVE ATTENTION

If I were to single out one commonality in the modes of engagement with the theatre artists I have observed, it would be the extraordinary quality of attention they demonstrate—to their materials, to each other, and to how all these relate in the process of creation.

Bogart (2001) refers to this quality of attention as "the only real gift I can offer an actor" (p. 74). Rather than thinking of attention as a talent some of us are gifted with (like the knack for remembering the lyrics of a song), she suggests that attention is something we deliberately provide to one another. Consider the director, as described in the introduction, observing student actors and offering images and questions to provoke and support their scene work. She also insists that attention is a human function, almost like a muscle: we can control it and get better at it.

Leon Ingulsrud (2006) gives an example from an open training in the Suzuki method at a SITI Company workshop for actors and directors. The Suzuki method is itself a form of rigorous attention to the body's precise movements and breathing. As he tells it, Leon's colleague leading the exercise suddenly stopped the exercise and told those observing, "Okay, everybody who's watching, pick somebody who you notice something about. Now give them the 'note,'" in other words, offer specific feedback on their movements that will help them to improve or extend their practice. The training became an exercise not only in the Suzuki method but also in giving of attention to one another.

One way to think about the methods for collective creation used by the SITI Company and others is as a means to deepen and extend the artists' attention to the elements of their work—questions, materials, and interactions with one another—as well as how these elements relate. The structures and tools of these methods serve as constant reminders to pay attention—and as aids for how we do so.

Listening, our first cue for action, is just one of the ways we pay attention. In *Games for Actors and Non-Actors*, Augusto Boal (1992) offers five categories of exercises: (1) feeling what we touch, (2) listening to what we hear, (3) dynamising several senses, (4) seeing what we look at, and (5) the memory of the senses. These remind me of a tool for honing our attention to student learning developed by Steve Seidel and colleagues at Project Zero.

The Collaborative Assessment Conference asks participants to examine a sample of work by a student without context (about the student, the assignment, the grade, etc.). The group begins by answering the apparently simple question, "What do you see?"—apparently simple because we are so accustomed to saying what we assume about the work or how we evaluate it rather than paying attention to what's actually there (Seidel, 1998).

The cue for action for educators is to consider the quality of our attention to the components of our own creation processes—to the materials, to the means through which we collectively create resources for our learning and instructional improvement, and to our colleagues during our interactions with them. It asks us to seek out and develop tools, like the Collaborative Assessment Conference or the Descriptive Review processes developed by Patricia Carini at the Prospect Center (Himley & Carini, 2000), to enhance the quality of our attention. It challenges us to use all of our attention to "give the note" to our collaborators in ways that enrich our individual and collective creation.

EMPHASIZE RIGOROUS CREATION

Theatre artists, even those most committed to collaborative methods, are much more likely to identify their groups as "companies" than "communities": the SITI Company, the Ghost Road Company, Pig Iron Theatre Company, Ping Chong & Company, and on and on. For educators, especially those who advocate for professional learning community, the use of the word *company* would smack of for-profit motives and hierarchies, antithetical to their primary commitment to collaboration that supports all of their students' learning. But what might educators learn from how theatre artists understand the word?

Companies make things, whether a car company making hatchbacks, a baking company cupcakes, a theatre company plays, or a dance company dances. The purpose for being together is always understood in relation to its product. For theatre artists, the product is always a performance, one that will embody and make available to others the exploration and discoveries that the company experiences in creating it.

The structures theatre artists employ, such as the Halprins' RSVP Cycles or Bogart and Landau's Composition steps, serve as means to achieve that product. They describe how, over time, a company initiates and sustains a process that results in a performance, often beginning with the identification of a question or problem that focuses and motivates subsequent stages of inquiry, exploration, and composition.

Theatre artists value the support they provide one another no less than teachers do. In their processes for collective creation, however, that support is manifest in how collaborators respond to and elaborate one another's offers ("Yes, and . . .") in order to create an improv piece, composition, or other performance-as-product. Missteps, risk taking, and even embarrassment are welcomed—not only because these are natural human responses but because they are essential to creation of the company's performances.

Reflection, too, is understood as a means for creating something: its value lies in its capacity to generate materials for the development of a piece for performance. Reflective practices, such as valuaction (from the RSVP Cycles) or Liz Lerman's (Lerman & Borstel, 2003) Critical Response Process thus point to very specific elements of "vocabulary"—moments, images, dialogue, and so forth—in the performers' activity that may contribute to the creation of a piece for performance. The effectiveness of any component of the process, whether an initiating question or problem, Composition exercise, or set of questions for reflection, is assessed in terms of how well it supports the creation of a performance-as-product.

The cue for action for TLGs is to recognize that there exists a variety of potential instructional and conceptual resources that they might create. Then to ask, how does our collective activity foster the creation of the resources that have the most meaning and use for us? The framework for collective creation (means-materials-modes of engagement) provides one tool for engaging in this critical self-reflection on process and products.

~

There is nothing antithetical about community and company, as the Joe Chaikin quote with which the chapter began declares. What brings these two images for practice together productively is how the participants, whether actors in a black box theatre or teachers in a staff room or school library, relate to the "work we all create," as J. C. from Park East High School put it.

Finally, it is a question of the mode of engagement we enact—a mode that describes how we relate to our colleagues and to our common activity. Will it be one that emphasizes validation or replication of what already exists? Or one that highlights listening, attention, and creation?

Appendix

Resources

The sections below offer references to some of the resources that have contributed to my understanding of collective creation—in the studio and in the teachers room. Many of these also provide specific tools to implement collective creation.

TEACHER LEARNING RESOURCES

Many teacher learning groups use inquiry cycles or teacher research cycles to organize their learning over time. In addition to the Evidence Process ("gears diagram") described in chapter 4, two other cycles are included in the book: the Cycle of Inquiry and Action in chapter 1 and the Cycle of Teacher Research, in chapter 6. For more about each, respectively, see: *The Evidence Process: A Collaborative Approach to Understanding and Improving Teaching and Learning* (Evidence Project Staff, 2001) and *Teaching as Inquiry: Asking Hard Questions to Improve Practice and Student Achievement* (Weinbaum et al., 2004); Kathleen Cushman's 1999 article, "The Cycle of Inquiry and Action: Essential Learning Communities," on the Coalition of Essential Schools website (www.essentialschools.org/resources/72); and Donald Freeman's *Doing Teacher Research: From Inquiry to Understanding* (1998).

One category of tools that has been especially useful in teacher learning groups is protocols for structuring conversations for specific purposes, including reflecting on an individual student's learning, providing feedback on a teacher's lesson or activity, and exploring problems of teaching and learning. Many such protocols are collected and described in these books: *The Power of Protocols: An Educator's Guide to Better Practice* (2nd ed.) by Joseph McDonald, Nancy Mohr, Alan Dichter, and Elizabeth McDonald (2007) and *Protocols for Professional Learning* by Lois Easton (2009). For many more protocols and resources for using them effectively, visit the School Reform Initiative website: www.schoolreforminitiative.org.

Two books that provide resources for organizing and facilitating conversations using protocols are: *Looking Together at Student Work* (2nd ed.) by Tina Blythe, David Allen, and Barbara S. Powell (2008) and *The Facilitator's Book of Questions: Tools for Looking Together at Student Work* by David Allen and Tina Blythe (2004).

Thinking routines, like Generate-Sort-Connect-Elaborate (chapter 6), are powerful and flexible tools for supporting generative thinking for students or teachers. You'll find many more thinking routines and resources for using them in *Making Thinking Visible: How to Promote Engagement, Understanding, and Independence for All Learners* by Ron Ritchhart, Mark Church, and Karin Morrison (2011).

The Making Learning Visible Project has developed many resources for understanding, documenting, and supporting individual and group learning, including the Protocol for Documenting Teachers' Reflections and the Exhibition of Teacher Learning described in chapter 6. *Visible Learners: Promoting Reggio-inspired Approaches in All Schools* by Daniel Gray Wilson, Mara Krechevsky, Ben Mardell, and Melissa Rivard (2013) provides more resources from and information about the project, as does the website: www.makinglearningvisible.org.

THEATRE ARTS RESOURCES

Anne Bogart and Tina Landau's (2005) *The Viewpoints Book: A Practical Guide to Viewpoints and Composition* is *the* manual for Composition exercises like those described in chapter 3. It also describes the Viewpoints training method used by Bogart's SITI Company. Bogart's essays on theatre, art, and life are collected in *And Then, You Act* (2007) and *A Director Prepares* (2001).

An important work on devised theatre, which is strongly related to collective creation, is *Devising Theatre: A Practical and Theoretical Handbook* by

Alison Oddey (1994). *Teachers Notes—Devising,* a small, accessible, and freely available guide to devising theatre by the Complicite company of London is available here: http://complicite.org/pdfs/Teachers_Notes_Devising_Pack.pdf.

Two books from the Routledge Performance Practitioners series offer excellent descriptions of the ideas and methods of two influential theatre artists and educators: *Anna Halprin* by Libby Worth and Helen Poyner (2004) and *Augusto Boal* by Frances Babbage (2004). Both books include exercises used by the artists. The book on Anna Halprin provides a clear exposition of the RSVP Cycles, which contributed powerfully to the development of the framework for collective creation in this book.

Liz Lerman's method for providing feedback on performances at all stages of development, referred to in chapter 6, is described in *Liz Lerman's Critical Response Process* by Lerman and John Borstel (2003). As the authors claim in their subtitle, this is a "method for getting useful feedback on anything you make, from dance to dessert."

There are many handbooks of theatre activities and theatre games, some specifically intended for use in schools. One that is strongly consistent with the ideas in this book and applicable to collective creation in many contexts is *The Performer's Guide to the Collaborative Process* by Shelia Kerrigan (2001).

I also recommend a video available on DVD called *Theater Games: Workshopping Body Language in Shakespeare* (Open University, 1999). Here you will find, among other gifted theatre teachers, the actress Fiona Shaw working with university acting students (see chapter 3).

Some theatre companies, including the SITI Company in New York City (www.siti.org), and the Pig Iron Theatre Company in Philadelphia (www.pigiron.org), offer workshops in their methods. Many of these are for more advanced theatre artists but some are open to those (like me) with little theatre or performance background. Each year, the Ko Festival of Performance (kofest.com) at Amherst College sponsors weeklong workshops by theatre companies, like the Ghost Road Company workshop described in chapter 3.

More and more theatre companies use collective creation methods. Their work is often performed in black box theatres and other nontraditional theatre spaces—usually with inexpensive ticket prices. See a performance soon!

References

AERA (2011). American Educational Research Association Annual Meeting, New Orleans, April 9.

Allen, D., & Blythe, T. (2004). *The facilitator's book of questions: Tools for looking together at student work*. New York: Teachers College Press.

Babbage, F. (2004). *Augusto Boal*. London: Routledge.

Ball, D. L. & Cohen, D. K. (1999). Developing practice, developing practitioners: Toward a practice-based theory of professional education. In G. Sykes and L. Darling-Hammond (Eds.), *Teaching as the learning profession: Handbook of policy and practice* (pp. 3–32). San Francisco: Jossey-Bass.

Barret, V. (2009). It's the teacher, stupid. Retrieved from www.forbes.com/2009/01/26/bill-gates-letter-tech-enter-cz_vb_0126billgates.html.

Bauriedel, Q. (2012). Interview (October 21).

Bausmth, J. M., & Barry, C. (2011). Revising professional learning communities to increase college readiness: The importance of pedagogical content knowledge. *Educational Researcher, 40*(4), 175–78.

Blythe, T., Allen, D., & Powell, B. S. (2008). *Looking together at student work* (2nd ed.). New York: Teachers College Press.

Blythe, T., & Associates. (1998). *The teaching for understanding guide*. San Francisco: Jossey-Bass.

Boal, A. (1979). *Theatre of the oppressed.* London: Pluto Press.

——. (1992). *Games for actors and non-actors.* London: Routledge.

——. (1995). *The rainbow of desire: The Boal method of theatre and therapy.* London: Routledge.

Bogart, A. (2001). *A director prepares: Seven essays on art and theatre.* New York: Routledge.

——. (2007). *And then, you act: Making art in an unpredictable world.* New York: Routledge.

Bogart, A., & Landau, T. (2005). *The viewpoints book: A practical guide to viewpoints and composition.* New York: Theatre Communications Group.

Brook, P. (1968). *The empty space.* New York: Touchstone.

Bryk, A. S., & Schneider, B. (2002). *Trust in schools: A core resource for improvement.* New York: Russell Sage Foundation.

Bryk, A. S., Sebring, P. B., Allensworth, E., Luppescu, S., & Easton, J. Q. (2010). *Organizing schools for improvement: Lessons from Chicago.* Chicago: University of Chicago Press.

Cahnmann-Taylor, M., Wooten, J., Souto-Manning, M., & Dice, J. (2009). The art and science of educational inquiry: Analysis of performance-based focus groups with novice bilingual teachers. *Teachers College Record, 111*(11), 2535–59.

Chaikin, J. (1991). *The presence of the actor.* New York: Theatre Communications Group.

Chen, M., Pulinkala, I., and Robinson, K. (2010). Polyphonic dynamics as educational practice. *Theatre Topics, 20*(2), 113–31.

Cochran-Smith, M., & Lytle, S. (2009). *Inquiry as a stance: Practitioner research for the next generation.* New York: Teachers College Press.

Complicite (n.d.). Teachers Notes—Devising. Available from http://complicite.org/pdfs/Teachers_Notes_Devising_Pack.pdf.

Crowther, F. (2011). *From school improvement to sustained capacity: The parallel leadership pathway.* Thousand Oaks, CA: Sage.

Croyden, M. (2003). *Conversations with Peter Brook, 1970–2000.* New York: Faber and Faber, Inc.

Cummings, S. T. (2006). *Remaking American theater: Charles Mee, Anne Bogart and the SITI Company*. Cambridge: Cambridge University Press.

Curry, M. (2008). Critical friends groups: The possibilities and limitations embedded in teacher professional communities aimed at instructional improvement and school reform. *Teachers College Record, 110*(4), 733–74.

Cushman, K. (1999). The cycle of inquiry and action: Essential learning communities. Providence, RI: Coalition of Essential Schools. Retrieved from www.essentialschools.org/resources/72.

Darling-Hammond, L. (2010). *The flat world and education: How America's commitment to equity will determine our future.* New York: Teachers College Press.

de Bono, E. (1990). *Lateral thinking: Creativity step by step.* New York: Harper & Row.

Dewey, J. (1900). *The school and society.* Chicago: University of Chicago Press.

——. (1910). *How we think.* Boston: Heath.

——. (1916). *Democracy and education: An introduction to the philosophy of education.* New York: The Free Press.

——. (1934). *Art as experience.* New York: Perigree.

Easton, L. B. (2009). *Protocols for professional learning.* Alexandria, VA: ASCD.

Egan, K. (1986). *Teaching as story telling: An alternative approach to teaching and curriculum in the elementary school.* Chicago: University of Chicago Press.

——. (1997). *The educated mind: How cognitive tools shape our understanding.* Chicago: University of Chicago Press.

Eisner, E. (1968). Qualitative intelligence and the act of teaching. In R. T. Hyman (Ed.), *Teaching: Vantage points of study* (pp. 359–368). Philadelphia, PA: Lippincott.

——. (2002). *The arts and the creation of mind.* New Haven, CT: Yale University Press.

Evans, B. (2006). Interview (June 23).

Evidence Project Staff (2001). *The Evidence Process: A collaborative approach to understanding and improving teaching and learning.* Cambridge, MA: Project Zero, Harvard Graduate School of Education.

Fendler, L. (2003). Teacher reflection in a hall of mirrors: Historical influences and political reverberations. *Educational Researcher, 32*(3), 16-25.

Fo, D. (1987). *The tricks of the trade.* London: Routledge.

Freeman, D. (1998). *Doing teacher research: From inquiry to understanding.* Pacific Grove, CA: Heinle & Heinle Publishers.

Fullan, M. (1993). *Change forces: Probing the depth of educational reform.* London: Falmer Press.

——. (2008). School leadership's unfinished agenda. *Education Week* (April 9), 36, 28.

Goffman, E. (1974). *Frame analysis: An essay on the organization of experience.* New York: Harper & Row.

Goodman, N. (1972). *Problems and projects.* Indianapolis, IN: Bobbs-Merrill.

——. (1978). *Ways of worldmaking.* Indianapolis, IN: Hackett Publishing Company.

Greene, M. (1986). The spaces of aesthetic education. *Journal of Aesthetic Education, 20*(4), 56–62.

——. (1995). *Releasing the imagination: Essays on education, the arts, and social change.* San Francisco: Jossey-Bass.

Griggs, T. (2001). Teaching as acting: Considering acting as epistemology and its use in teaching and teacher preparation. *Teacher Education Quarterly, 28*(2), 23–37.

Grossman, P., Compton, C., Igra, D., Ronfeldt, M., Shahan, E., & Williamson, P. (2009). Teaching practice: A cross-professional perspective. *Teachers College Record, 11*(9). Retrieved from www.tcrecord.org.

Grossman, P., Wineburg, S., & Woolworth, S. (2001). Toward a theory of teacher community. *Teachers College Review, 103*(6), 942–1012.

Hall, R. (1996). Representation as shared activity: Situated cognition and Dewey's cartography of experience. *The Journal of the Learning Sciences, 5*(3), 209–38.

Halprin, A. (1995). *Moving towards life: Five decades of transformational dance,* ed. R. Kaplan. Middletown, CT: Wesleyan University Press.

Halprin, L., & Burns, J. (1974). *Taking part: A workshop approach to collective creativity.* Cambridge, MA: MIT Press.

Hargreaves, A., & Dawe, R. (1990). Paths of professional development: Contrived collegiality, collaborative culture, and the case of peer coaching. *Teaching and Teacher Education, 6*(3), 227–41.

Hargreaves, A., & Fullan, M. (2012). *Professional capital: Transforming teaching in every school.* New York: Teachers College Press.

Himley, M., & Carini, P. (2000). *From another angle: Children's strengths and school standards: The Prospect Center's descriptive review of a child.* New York: Teachers College Press.

Hord, S. (1997). *Professional learning communities: Communities of continuous inquiry and improvement.* Austin, TX: Southwest Educational Development Laboratory.

Horn, I. S. (2010). Teaching replays, teaching rehearsals, and re-visions of practice: Learning from colleagues in a mathematics teacher community. *Teachers College Record. 112*(1), 225–59.

Ingulsrud, L. (2006). Interview (June 23).

Jackson, P. (1998). *John Dewey and the lessons of art.* New Haven, CT: Yale University Press.

John, P. D. (2006). Lesson planning and the student teacher: Re-thinking the dominant model. *Journal of Curriculum Studies, 38*(4), 483–98.

Kahneman, D. (2012). *Thinking, fast and slow.* New York: Farrar, Straus and Giroux.

Kerrigan, S. (2001). *The performer's guide to the collaborative process.* Portsmouth, NH: Heinemann.

Knowles, R. (2004). *Reading the material theatre.* Cambridge: Cambridge University Press.

Konigsburg, E. L. (1967). *From the mixed-up files of Mrs. Basil E. Frankweiler.* New York: Atheneum.

Koretz, D. (2009). *Measuring up: What educational testing really tells us.* Cambridge, MA: Harvard University Press.

Labaree, D. (2010). *Someone has to fail: The zero-sum game of public schooling.* Cambridge, MA: Harvard University Press.

Lagemann, E. C. (2000). *An elusive science: The troubling history of education research.* Chicago: University of Chicago Press.

Lave, J., & Wenger, E. (1991). *Situated learning: Legitimate peripheral participation*. Cambridge: Cambridge University Press.

Lemov, D. (2010). *Teach like a champion*. Press release. Retrieved from http://teachlikeachampion.wiley.com.

Lerman, L., & Borstel, J. (2003). *Liz Lerman's critical response process: A method for getting useful feedback on anything you make, from dance to dessert*. Takoma Park, MD: Liz Lerman's Dance Exchange.

Lewis, J. M. (2011). The role of rehearsal in learning to teach mathematics: Learning from clinical psychology and pastoral education. American Educational Research Association Annual Meeting. New Orleans (April).

Little, J. W. (1982). Norms of collegiality and experimentation: Workplace conditions of social success. *American Educational Research Journal, 19*(3), 325–40.

——. (1990). The persistence of privacy: Autonomy and initiative in teachers' professional relations. *Teachers College Record, 91*(4), 509–36.

——. (2003). Inside teacher community: Representations of classroom practice. *Teachers College Record, 105*(6), 913–45.

——. (2007). Teachers' accounts of classroom experience as a resource for professional learning and instructional decision making. *Yearbook of the National Society for the Study of Education, 106*(1), 217–40.

Louis, K. S., Kruse, S. D., & Marks, H. M. (1996). Schoolwide professional community. In F. Newmann & Associates (Eds.), *Authentic achievement: Restructuring schools for intellectual quality* (pp. 179–203). San Francisco: Jossey-Bass.

Louis, K. S. Creating and sustaining professional communities. In A.M. Blankstein (Ed.), *Sustaining professional learning communities* (pp. 41–58). San Francisco: Corwin Press.

Lunenberg, F. C. (2010). Total Quality Management applied to schools. *Schooling, 1*(1), 1–5.

MacBurney, S., & Complicite. (2003). *Complicite: Plays 1*. London: Methuen Drama.

Marshall, K. (2009). *Rethinking teacher supervision and evaluation: How to work smart, build collaboration, and close the achievement gap*. San Francisco: Jossey-Bass.

McDonald, J. P., Mohr, N., Dichter, A., & McDonald, E. C. (2007). *The power of protocols: An educator's guide to better practice* (2nd ed.). New York: Teachers College Press.

McDonough, E. G. (2003). Investigation of factors contributing to the success of cross-functional teams. *Journal of Product Innovation Management, 17*(3), 221–35.

McLaughlin, M. W., & Talbert, J. E. (2001). *Professional communities and the work of high school teaching*. Chicago: University of Chicago Press.

———. (2006). *Building school-based teacher learning communities: Strategies to improve student achievement*. New York: Teachers College Press.

Mee, C., & Bogart, A. (2007). BAMDialogue. Brooklyn Academy of Music, Brooklyn, NY. (October 10).

Meirink, J. A., Meijer, P. C., Verloop, N. (2007). A closer look at teachers' individual learning in collaborative settings. *Teachers and Teaching: Theory and Practice, 13*(2), 145–64.

MetLife, Inc. (2011). *MetLife Survey of the American Teacher: Preparing students for college and career*. New York: MetLife, Inc.

Moje, E. B. (2011). Learning from the professions: Innovative designs in teacher education that draw on preparation for practice in other professions through clinical rounds. American Educational Research Association Annual Meeting. New Orleans (April).

Nelson, T. H., Slavit, D., & Deuel, A. (2012). Two dimensions of an inquiry stance towards student-learning data. *Teachers College Record, 114*. Retrieved from www .tcrecord.org.

Noon, K. (2011). Interview (July 29).

Oddey, A. (1994). *Devising theatre: A practical and theoretical handbook*. London: Routledge.

Open University. (1999). *Theater games: Workshopping body language in Shakespeare*. New York: Films Media Group. DVD.

Perkins, D., & Blythe, T. (1994). Putting understanding up front. *Educational Leadership, 51*(5), 4–7.

Project Zero & Reggio Children. (2001). Making learning visible: Children as individual and group learners. Reggio Emilia, Italy: Reggio Emilia Publications.

Rabinow, P. (2003). *Anthropos today: Reflections on modern equipment*. Princeton, NJ: Princeton University Press.

———. (2011). *The accompaniment: Assembling the contemporary*. Chicago: University of Chicago Press.

Randel, A. E., & Jaussi, K. S. (2003). Functional background identity, diversity, and individual performance in cross-functional teams. *Academy of Management Journal, 46*(6), 763–44.

Ritchhart, R., Church, M., & Morrison, K. (2011). *Making thinking visible: How to promote engagement, understanding, and independence for all learners*. San Francisco: Jossey-Bass.

Rodgers, C. (2002). Defining reflection: Another look at John Dewey and reflective thinking. *Teachers College Record, 104*(2), 842–66.

Rogoff, B., Baker-Sennett, J., Lacasa, P., & Goldsmith, D. (1995). Development through participation in sociocultural activity. In J. J. Goodnow, P. J. Miller, & F. Kessel (Eds.), *Cultural practices as contexts for development* (pp. 45–65). San Francisco: Jossey-Bass.

Sallis, E. (2002). *Total quality management in education* (3rd ed.) London: Routledge.

Sarason, S. B. (1999). *Teaching as a performing art*. New York: Teachers College Press.

Sawyer, R. K. (2003). *Improvised dialogues: Emergence and creativity in conversation*. Westport, CT: Ablex.

Schreck, M. K. (2009). *Transformers: Creative teachers for the 21st century*. Thousand Oaks, CA: Corwin Press.

Scott, S. E. (2008). Rehearsing for ambitious instruction in the university classroom: A case study of a literacy methods course. American Educational Research Association Annual Meeting. New York (March).

Seidel, S. (1998). Wondering to be done. In D. Allen (Ed.), *Assessing student learning: From grading to understanding* (pp. 21–39). New York: Teachers College Press.

Shagoury, R., & Power, B. M. (2012). *Living the questions: A guide for teacher-researchers* (2nd ed.). Portland, ME: Stenhouse Publishers.

Shulman, L. (1987). Knowledge and teaching: Foundations of the new reform. *Harvard Education Review, 57*(1), 1–21.

Spry, L. (1994). Structures of power: Toward a theatre of liberation. In M. Schutzman & J. Cohen-Cruz (Eds.). *Playing Boal: Theatre, therapy, activism*, pp. 171–184. London: Routledge.

Stevens, W. D., & Kahne, J. (2006). *Professional communities and instructional improvement practices: A study of small high schools in Chicago.* Chicago: Consortium on Chicago School Research, University of Chicago.

Tauber, R. T., & Mester, C. S. (2007). *Acting lessons for teachers: Using performance skills in the classroom* (2nd ed.). Westport, CT: Praeger.

Vescio, V., Ross, D., & Adams, A. (2008). A review of research on the impact of professional learning communities on teaching practice and student learning. *Teaching and Teacher Education, 24*(1), 80–91.

Vygotsky, L. S. (1978). *Mind in society.* Cambridge, MA: Harvard University Press.

Wei, R. C., Darling-Hammond, L., Andree, A., Richardson, N., Orphanos, S. (2009). *Professional learning in the learning profession: A status report on teacher development in the United States and abroad.* Dallas, TX: National Staff Development Council.

Weinbaum, A., Allen, D., Blythe, T., Simon, K., Seidel, S., & Rubin, C. (2004). *Teaching as inquiry: Asking hard questions to improve practice and student achievement.* New York: Teachers College Press.

Wekwerth, M. (2011). *Daring to play: A Brecht companion.* London: Routledge.

Wells, G. (1999). *Dialogic inquiry: Towards a sociocultural practice and theory in education.* Cambridge: Cambridge University Press.

Wenger, E. (1998). *Communities of practice: Learning, meaning, and identity.* Cambridge: Cambridge University Press.

Wertsch, J. V. (1991). *Voices of the mind: A sociocultural approach to mediated action.* Cambridge, MA: Harvard University Press.

Wilson, D. G., Krechevsky, M., Mardell, B., & Rivard, M. (2013). *Visible learners: Promoting Reggio-inspired approaches in all schools.* San Francisco: Jossey-Bass.

Wilson, D., Perkins, D. N., Bonnet, D., Miani, C., & Unger, C. (2005). *Learning at work: Research lessons on leading learning in the workplace.* Cambridge MA: Presidents and Fellows of Harvard College.

Windschitl, M., Thompson, J., Braaten, M. (2011). Ambitious pedagogy by novice teachers: Who benefits from tool-supported collaborative inquiry and why? *Teachers College Record, 113*(7). Retrieved from www.tcrecord.org.

Wood, D. R. (2007). Teachers' learning communities: Catalyst for change or infrastructure for the status quo? *Teachers College Record, 109*(3), 699–739.

Worth, A., & Poynor, H. (2004). *Anna Halprin.* London: Routledge.

Zeichner, K. M., & Liston, D. P. (1996). *Reflective teaching: An introduction.* Mahwah, NJ: Erlbaum.